'Excuse me,' Nathan enquired. 'Might I ask what's going on?'

'Only way out . . .' Lucius pointed down. The soldiers had reached the bedroom door and were thumping on it, trying to force it open. 'Or maybe you like to stay and fight?' Charlie examined the escape route: there was a sheer drop right down to the ocean. 'Even if you fall, you be safe,' Lucius reassured him. 'Water very deep.'

But Jake's attention had been caught by something else: a pale blue dress with gold embroidery around its hem and neckline lay over a chair. It belonged to a different era entirely. 'I – I know that,' he stammered. 'Topaz was wearing it when I last saw her. Is this her room?' he asked the soldier, now looking around with keen interest. He noticed a long thick chain: one end was fastened to the wall; the other had a brace with a lock fitted on it. 'Was she tied up here?' asked Jake, going pale. He gritted his teeth. 'Where is she? We demand to know.'

'She has gone!' Lucius insisted firmly, throwing out the second rope. 'To Herculaneum.'

'Herculaneum?' asked Jake.

'It's on the mainland,' Charlie explained. 'Just north of Pompeii. There's a wonderful library there.'

'What's she doing in a library?' Jake continued his cross-examination, but the bangs on the door were becoming more urgent: the casing of the top bolt had almost come loose and the bottom was on its way.

'Questions later, perhaps . . .?' Charlie leaped up onto the windowsill. 'Jake, shall we?' he asked, taking hold of the first rope.

Jake followed his lead, but then looked down and saw the drop. 'You're joking!' he gasped: they were higher than any cliff he had ever dared to peer over.

'Any time you like,' Nathan remarked sarcastically, one eye on the rattling door.

Jake grabbed hold of the second rope, took a deep breath and started to climb down. As soon as he was below the window – the top floor hung out over the sea – it swung sideways and he nearly lost his grip. When Nathan took hold of the same rope above him, it swung back the other way. Jake clung on for his life, and continued to inch his way down.

The four of them abseiled down the sheer cliff face, Charlie and Lucius on one rope, Jake and Nathan on the other. Suddenly there was a great splintering of wood from above and the sound of a door crashing open. A moment later, ten war-like

faces – each protected by a bronze, slit-eyed mask – appeared through the aperture above, and within seconds, the soldiers were aiming bows and arrows.

'I see you at the bottom,' Lucius announced. 'Hurry!'

Jake watched in amazement as he kicked away from the cliff and let go of the rope. He threw his arms into the air and dived, yelling as he plummeted earthwards. Halfway down – simply to show off, it appeared – he tucked into a somersault before finally entering the water, his body faultlessly straight, creating a perfect concentric ripple far, far below.

'No way – I'm not doing that,' Jake stammered, picking up speed down the rope, burning his hands as an arrow from above whistled past.

Nathan was also appalled, but for different reasons. 'Just *one* somersault?' he sneered. 'No twist or pike? What an amateur.' And now he also let go and threw himself out with a flourish, attempting two revolutions *and* a twist on the way down. In truth, despite his bravado, he was not as elegant as Lucius, and hit the water at an awkward angle. Charlie grimaced.

Now, whole swarms of arrows were flying

through the air and, to make matters worse, the enemy were starting to hack through the ropes. Jake and Charlie knew that jumping was their only option.

'I'll count to three,' Charlie shouted over to Jake, ducking his head as a missile sailed past, 'and we'll go together.' Jake nodded grimly. He could feel goose-bumps tightening the skin around his neck. 'Keep as straight as you can. One, two' – Jake closed his eyes in prayer – 'three.'

He opened his eyes again, pushed away from the cliff, and let go. An exquisite chill shot up his spine; colour and light flashed all around him. He heard an arrow pass by in slow motion, then gravity took over as he plunged down, accelerating towards certain death. The ocean shot towards him and he hit the surface. His first thought was that it wasn't water at all: it felt like solid ground, sending an agonizing jolt up his back. But then he lost his hearing, and everything was cold, dark and blue. Within seconds he was swimming up towards the glinting surface. The moment he popped up into the sunshine again, another clutch of arrows whistled past into the water.

'Here!' Nathan was shouting. 'Soldier boy wants

us to go this way.' He pointed towards the mouth of a cave leading under the cliff. 'Apparently it goes through to the harbour.'

Lucius was holding onto a rock, grinning his dazzling smile. 'Let's go!' he urged them.

Nathan, Jake and Charlie – who was not at home in the water, and had swallowed a good deal of it – swam after him into a cavern, dripping with stalactites, that twisted its way into the mountain.

'Topaz told me you come,' Lucius explained, 'and that I help you. I wait three days.'

'The pleasure is all ours,' said Nathan with an insincere smile.

'How is it you speak English?' Charlie asked, holding his head above the water with difficulty.

'We all learn English,' Lucius stated. 'The magistra commands it. Also' – he smiled – 'I had extra lessons from Topaz.'

Jake looked across at him; he wasn't sure if he'd heard correctly in the echoey tunnel, but there was a distinct warmth in the soldier's voice.

'And the magistra is your commander?' Charlie wondered.

'Not any more.' Lucius laughed heartily.

'And what's your connection with Topaz?' Nathan asked tersely.

Lucius didn't answer the question, but instead asked him, 'You swim all right?'

'I swim just fine, thank you,' the American replied firmly. 'In fact I've won a load of prizes for my skill in the water.' He demonstrated by switching to his best front crawl and taking off at speed.

'Your friend is very proud!' Lucius laughed again, the sound echoing around the chamber. As it died away, they became aware of other voices behind them. Charlie looked back and saw a sharp-prowed boat carrying five or six soldiers, their strange hooked-nose masks catching the light.

'The Hydra never give up!' Lucius replied. 'We are trained to fight to the death.'

They all turned and swam quickly along the channel.

'I take it the Hydra are your amiable friends from the villa upstairs?' Charlie spluttered. 'Good name,' he commented to Jake. 'From Greek mythology: the evil serpent with many heads.'

'Not friends any more!' Lucius shouted as more missiles, this time identified by Charlie as *pila* –

javelins – and *spincula* – iron darts – started to fly through the air.

Finally the four swimmers made it through to the harbour. They hauled themselves up out of the water and picked their way quickly across the rocks and onto the rickety wooden pier where the *Conqueror* was waiting. Mr Drake, who was sitting anxiously on the yardarm, squawked – first with delight, when he saw them coming, then with terror when he realized what was going on.

'That is your ship?' Lucius asked, pulling a face. '*Exigua est*. It's small.'

'What does he want?' Nathan shook his head at the others. 'An Atlantic clipper? A Norse longship? Who is this strange person and what is his problem? All aboard – I'll cast off.'

Jake and Charlie climbed the gangplank, while Lucius, in a ridiculous manoeuvre, crouched and vaulted up, twisting in a salto and landing with a flourish on the prow.

Their pursuers emerged from the cave, firing another volley of missiles. Then, to make matters worse, they saw three more vessels, each with its own complement of soldiers, rounding the head-land.

'I hate to make the bad news' – Lucius nodded towards the soldiers – 'but we now surrounded.'

Nathan jumped aboard, drew up the gangplank and took the helm. 'You might look the part – the tough physique, the dimple in the chin and the teeth that I can see my reflection in – but we've been doing this for years. And this ship may be small, but it's certainly not *exigua*!' To prove his point, Nathan fired up the engine, set the gear and took off, sending Lucius tottering along the deck. A group of locals, mending nets, watched in amazement. The *Conqueror* smashed into the three boatloads of muscle and careered off across the bay.

As the ship sped on, Lucius clung to the rail, amazed and terrified in equal measure, muttering about *magicus*.

'What's he saying?' Jake asked.

'He is wondering if this is magic,' Charlie translated.

'*Or if it is Neptune's craft*,' Nathan added with a roll of his eyes, before turning to the soldier with a shrug. 'Neptune, that's right – friends in *low* places.'

Once the ship had reached the open sea and Vulcano was just a hazy shape on the horizon

behind them, Nathan throttled back and – in his most serious voice – called a meeting.

'So Topaz has gone to Herculaneum?' he asked. 'You're absolutely sure of that?'

Lucius nodded. 'Two days ago, with the magistra and Leopardo.'

'And *who* is Leopardo exactly?' Nathan enquired. 'Apart from someone who needs a good hiding.'

Jake braced himself for the answer.

'Brother of Topaz.' Lucius uttered the unthinkable, but then corrected himself slightly: 'Half-brother. They hate each other.'

'They've gone to Herculaneum for what reason?'

'The magistra—'

'Could we just call her Agata?' Nathan interjected testily. 'That name is starting to grate. And seeing as you're not working for her any more . . .'

Lucius eyeballed him defiantly, before continuing, 'The magistra was picking up a – *quid dico?* – *sarcina* . . . a package.'

'A package?' Nathan jumped in. 'What package?' Lucius shrugged, so he turned to Charlie. 'Do you think it's atomium?' It was Charlie's turn to shrug. Nathan continued the cross-examination: 'Where exactly was she picking up this package?'

'From the *theatrum*. The theatre.'

'The theatre?' Nathan snorted. 'This is all getting a little far-fetched.'

'Believe me. Don't believe me.' Lucius held up his hands. 'No difference.'

'Actually there *is* a theatre in Herculaneum,' Charlie chipped in. 'It's as famous as the library.' He turned to Lucius. 'I have to ask – why are you helping us?'

'I help you – you help Topaz.'

At this admission, Jake felt another twinge of uncertainty, a premonition of something. He found himself asking the question but didn't really want to know the answer. 'And why do you want to help Topaz?'

Lucius showed his gleaming teeth. 'Because I love her.'

This was bad enough for Jake, but his second declaration was worse:

'And she loves me.'

Nathan was also appalled at the notion. 'Now hold on a minute,' he said, pulling himself up to his full height and pushing his chin out. 'That's my sister you're talking about. I don't know the first thing about you. How old are you?'

'Seventeen,' Lucius replied proudly. He was older than all of them.

Nathan didn't like that at all. 'Well, that's *too* old for her,' he retorted.

Lucius squared up to him: they were of equal height, each as striking as the other, though Lucius was the bulkier of the two. 'I not care you do not like,' he smouldered. 'I risk my life on Vulcano,' he said, jerking his thumb back at the island behind them. 'Everything I had, gone. Now, I am *reus* . . . a criminal . . . *me quaerent* – I will be hunted down.' With a scowl, he put his face close up to Nathan's.

'Let's not be overdramatic!' Nathan grimaced, refusing to back away. 'You made choices – nothing to do with Topaz.'

'All right, you two,' said Charlie, prising them apart. 'Let's cool down a little.' He whispered in Nathan's ear, 'He's obviously just an ordinary chap that Topaz roped in to help. Go a little easier on him.' Charlie turned back to Lucius. 'It was very kind of you to assist us, whatever the reason. Is there anything else you can tell us about Topaz?'

Lucius reluctantly took a step back, loosened his breastplate, reached his hand inside and produced a small package from a secret pocket. 'This is from

her,' he announced, placing it in Charlie's hand.

All three History Keepers looked at each other in disbelief. 'You've had that all this time?' Nathan grunted with irritation. 'Why didn't you give it to us sooner?'

'I give it to you now!' Lucius retreated, shaking his head and muttering to himself.

As the other two crowded round, Charlie quickly unwrapped the package. It contained a small wax tablet inscribed with two lines that had obviously been written in a hurry.

Charlie read it aloud: '*Meet me nine a.m., the ides of May, Pons Fabricius . . .*' He took a deep breath. '*Code purple.*'

The three agents exchanged glances. Nathan reached over and took the tablet. 'It's her writing, all right,' he commented. '*The ides of May* – that's the fifteenth, two days away. Is the Pons Fabricius in Herculaneum?'

'Negative,' said Charlie, pushing his glasses up his nose. 'The Pons Fabricius is one of the oldest and most famous bridges in the world: it crosses over to the Tiber Island. It's in Rome.'

'Rome?' Nathan threw up his hands and turned on Lucius accusingly. 'You said she'd gone to Herculaneum?'

'She tell me that!' Lucius replied, and once again they squared up to each other like a couple of stags.

'Just calm down, you two,' Charlie interceded a second time. 'It's quite possible that she has gone to Herculaneum and *then* to Rome. It's on the way there, halfway up the coast. Nathan, I suggest we continue north in any case. We can discuss our destination at dinner. I'll go down and rustle something up. All that excitement has made me famished.'

At length, everyone nodded in agreement. Charlie disappeared below deck, whistling happily. Mr Drake followed quickly, not wishing to be left with the warring factions. Nathan returned to the helm, and Jake and Lucius went to opposite ends of the ship to stew over their various misfortunes. After staring out at the sun setting over the Tyrrhenian Sea for a while, Jake glanced back at his rival.

Lucius was tall, impossibly good-looking, a soldier and, most crucially, nearly three years older than him. For all Jake knew, he was probably kind-hearted too (Jake couldn't imagine why Topaz would be interested in him if he wasn't). In Jake's eyes, this man – it pained him deeply to admit it – was the whole package.

*

Charlie returned from the galley fifteen minutes later, carrying a tray of delicious food. 'Simple Mediterranean fare.' He sighed blissfully as he set it down on the table. 'It's the best!' He indicated each bowl in turn: 'Olive tapenade, yoghurt and fresh figs, sorrel and chicory salad, home-made chickpea falafels and this delicious rye bread I bought this morning in Messina.'

In truth, Jake had lost his appetite a little; but Charlie's meal was, as always, incredibly tasty, and soon every last morsel was being fought over by the four of them.

When the plates were empty, Charlie fetched the pudding. 'I may have surpassed myself here – date soufflé with poppy seeds,' he announced proudly as he set down the dish. Out of earshot of Lucius he whispered, 'It's basically cheesecake.'

They tucked in – Lucius was particularly impressed – and hostilities began to thaw, though not for long.

'Which one of you is' – Lucius spat out a seed as he tried to recall the name – 'Yake?'

'*Jake* – that's me. Did Topaz have a message for me?' Jake asked excitedly.

'No.' Lucius shook his head and took another mouthful. The other three had to wait for him to chew and swallow before he carried on, 'You enemy number one, they say. I am surprised . . . I expect someone more' – he turned to examine Jake and even went so far as to feel his biceps, which were by no means bulging – 'more *infigo*, more *athletico*.'

Jake ignored the slur, focusing instead on the bombshell. For the second time that day he felt as if someone had delivered him a body blow. 'Enemy number one?' he stammered. 'What do you mean?'

'You make the magistra's brother, Prince Xander Zeldt, blind. There is money on your head. Now is money on *my* head too. Maybe I enemy number one now,' he declared with a laugh. No one joined in.

'Zeldt was blinded?' Jake found himself asking, as if in a dream.

'They say he never sees again.' Lucius shrugged as he helped himself to the last spoonful of pudding. 'Though he gone to see a special doctor.'

Jake took in the news. He had last seen Prince Zeldt, Topaz's infinitely evil uncle and scourge of the History Keepers' Secret Service, on board the *Lindwurm*, during his mission to try and save her. It

was because of his calamitously misguided intervention that Topaz had had no choice but to set fire to Zeldt's cabinet of embalmed heads – which had exploded in his face. Jake did not know he had been blinded – and though he certainly deserved to be punished (after all, he did try and destroy Renaissance Europe with deadly bubonic plague), Jake was appalled to discover that he himself was now a wanted man.

'I wouldn't worry about it, Jake,' Charlie jumped in quickly. 'We've all had prices on our head. They're two a penny these days. If anything, it's a compliment.' He turned to Lucius. 'Any idea where Zeldt went to see this doctor?'

'A place called . . .' He had trouble recalling the name. 'Vindobona?'

Charlie whispered to the others, 'That's the old name for Vienna. No doubt he's gone to the nineteenth century, when ocular surgery took off. At least he is out of the way.'

'And did he have that she-devil Mina Schlitz with him?' Nathan butted in.

At the mention of her name, Jake felt another jolt of anxiety. She was Zeldt's right-hand woman, an ice-blooded assassin. Her one concession to

humanity was her love for her pet snake – though that had perished in the fire on the *Lindwurm*. Lucius knew immediately who they were talking about and told them that she had gone with her master. 'She and the magistra did not like each other . . .'

'Can you imagine those two together?' Nathan drawled. 'Conviviality soup.'

As evening fell, the three agents discussed where they should head first: Herculaneum or Rome. Jake wanted to go straight to the latter and start looking for Topaz, but Charlie reasoned – successfully – that as their proposed rendezvous with her wasn't for another day and a half, and as they would sail by Herculaneum anyway, they might as well go there first and try and find out more about this mysterious *package* that Agata Zeldt was picking up at the theatre.

When their course was agreed, Charlie took the helm (he loved being at the wheel at night). Mr Drake tried to stay awake on his shoulder, while Nathan and Jake sat down to enjoy the balmy evening and the celestial lightshow. Jake never tired of the magic of the star-rise.

Lucius had fallen asleep on deck. His bulky frame and handsome face were twitching as he took

on some invisible foe in his dreams. Jake and Nathan examined him in silence.

'I don't believe Topaz is in love with him,' Nathan said finally. 'She doesn't fall in love – it's not her style.' Another few minutes passed before he spoke again. He turned to Jake very seriously and announced, 'I love my sister, but she's as complicated as a box of frogs, you know.'

Jake nodded and half smiled. He was in no doubt that Nathan meant this as a warning. He didn't reply.

The *Conqueror* sailed on into the night.

12 THE FLAME-HAIRED SIBYL

A convoy of three dark carriages rattled across the countryside. Each was pulled by a team of four black stallions – savage beasts with wild eyes and flaring nostrils, their coats shining in the moonlight. At the gates of a farm a night watchman stared – first bleary-eyed, then with growing alarm – as they charged towards him. The earth rumbled; he heard the vicious cries of the drivers, the crack of whips, and the vehicles thundered past, spattering him with gravel and leaving a cloud of choking dust in their wake. They tore over the brow of the hill and rattled down towards the flickering lights of a sprawling city.

The carriages flew down dark and narrow city streets, careless of both people and animals that got in their way; two wheels lifted off the ground as they

veered round corners. They ascended a steep hill and at last clattered through an archway into the large court-yard of a huge villa and came to a halt. Two colossal gates, each decorated with the motif of a giant bird, were closed behind them with a resounding clang.

For just a second there was no sound but the panting and snorting of horses; then, with lightning efficiency, a platoon of guards filed out into the courtyard, standing to attention. The driver of the first carriage and his companion, both with the distinctive grey breastplates and feathered shoulders of the Hydra, jumped out, opened the carriage door and set down the step, before bowing and stepping back respectfully.

First to emerge from the silky blackness of the vehicle's interior was a tall youth, long-limbed and athletic. He too wore the uniform of the Hydra, but each element – breastplate, shoulder pads, boots and helmet – had been finely wrought in gold and ebony. He had a mane of perfectly straight blond hair and a cruel smile. A cloak hung down his back – a luxurious fur with the spots of a leopard.

He descended in one lithe movement, took off his gloves, then inclined his head as another figure appeared, ghost-like. It was a lady, tall and imperious,

in a dress of shimmering darkness and a black veil that covered her head and shoulders. Through this, only the faintest glimpse of a pale face could be seen, framed by flame-coloured hair. Her whole being instilled a feeling of dread. It even chilled the blood of her loyal soldiers. As she stepped down, their backs seemed to stiffen in unison and their faces set in expressions of terror.

She placed a languid hand on her companion's shoulder – Leopardo was both her son *and* her lieutenant – and whispered something to him, then turned and swept towards the villa.

Leopardo strode over to the second carriage, opened the door and spoke to its occupant, who now descended – a portly middle-aged man swaddled in a cloak. He cast his tired, puffy eyes around the courtyard as Leopardo went on to the third carriage. This one was locked with chains. With a sadistic smile he peered through its latticed sides and snarled something to the figure inside.

Like a bride of darkness, Agata Zeldt glided down a wide, torch-lit passageway into the heart of the villa, her heels clicking on the marble floor. As she passed, slaves froze, trembling, their heads bowed low.

Ahead of her, huge double doors of ivory and gold swung open.

Beyond them, a vast ballroom was lit by low braziers of flickering flames. It housed a giant cage – an indoor aviary divided into two compartments. The left-hand section was inhabited by a solitary prisoner chained to a post, dressed in the uniform of the Hydra. He was stocky and muscular but now bruised and unkempt after days of incarceration. He lifted his head as Agata entered, but she did not return his gaze; instead she strode over to the right-hand compartment, where three massive birds – the finest and deadliest of all her flock – were squawking excitedly.

A smile lit up her face behind her silken shroud, and she put her pale hands between the bars and waited for the birds to come to her. They swooped down, flapping their wings in delight, nipping her with their beaks and fighting for her attention. Entranced by their devotion, Agata sighed, making her veil billow out in front of her.

She withdrew her hands and clapped to summon the birdkeeper. A moment later, a paunchy man wearing a blood-splattered leather apron lumbered out of the darkness. In his chubby hands he carried a basket, which he held up to his mistress.

Agata examined the contents: it was crawling with living things – rats, mice, thin snakes and monster-sized beetles – all slithering, scratching and scrambling on top of each other in a diabolical soup. Undaunted, she reached in and took hold of a fat rodent with a thick, hairless tail and passed it through the bars. The birds pounced immediately, squawking with pleasure, one snapping off its head, another tearing at its body, pulling it to pieces, their necks bobbing as the lumps of flesh went down.

'You poor things are starving,' she said. 'But not to worry – dinner's coming.' Now she went over to the other compartment. She stopped in front of the prisoner and removed her veil. As it slipped off, it made a soft hiss. Seeing her face, the unfortunate soldier did a double-take, as if he were looking at the Gorgon herself.

At first glance, Agata's face was handsome – proud, with a high forehead. But further scrutiny revealed something more unsettling: the features – nose, eyes, mouth, chin – all striking individually, did not *quite* fit together. It appeared as if they had been taken apart and carefully reassembled like Frankenstein's bride, leaving the faintest reminders of surgery.

Her age was incalculable; like her brother, she could have been forty or sixty, or even older. Her skin – which was pulled tight, erasing all her lines – was pale and translucent like marble, and showed a faint network of blue veins. One of her eyes was blue; the other was slate grey, and slightly duller than its twin. Most striking of all was her red hair, which was as rich and dry as burnt copper.

'Do you know why you are here?' she asked.

'No, Magistra,' the prisoner replied, his voice cracking.

The door opened and Leopardo strode in and came to stand by his mother.

Agata reached into her cloak and produced a small bundle of scrolls, speaking once more to the prisoner. 'This was the last batch of letters you delivered to me – three Imperial missives sent from Capri to Rome – along with a further two from the Senate back to Capri. Five dispatches in all.'

'That's correct, Magistra. As usual, I intercepted them at the port of Surrentum and made the necessary substitutions.'

'So would you like to explain to me about the remaining communiqués?'

'No, Magistra. I got them all.'

Agata stared at the soldier as beads of sweat formed on his brow. She held out her hand and Leopardo deposited into it another bundle of scrolls. The sight of them made the prisoner shudder.

'My son retrieved these from a messenger already halfway to the city. If these letters, from Tiberius himself, had arrived at their destination, all our work would have been in vain.'

'I . . . I don't understand how it could happen,' the soldier stammered. 'I had ten men watching the port.'

The birds peered through the bars of their compartment with mounting excitement, knowing that some treat was in the offing. Their bloodthirsty caws become noisier and shriller as they poked their heads through, flapping their wings in anticipation.

'History is about to be rewritten,' Agata rasped through the bars, 'but your incompetence has caused you to miss the show.' She nodded at Leopardo, who stepped over and slid out the grille that separated the two compartments. At once the vultures took off towards the soldier. He cried out desperately, pulling at his shackles as they circled above his head, savouring the exquisite moment. Then, as one, they swooped down.

Leopardo clutched his mother's shoulders in delight. Agata's mouth fell open as she watched the spectacle, clasping her hands together as the screams of man and birds mingled in one satanic cacophony. A tiny fleck of blood flew across the chamber and landed on Agata's white cheek. She shivered as it struck her, but she did not wipe it off. Within a minute, the man's cries had died away; only the vultures could be heard, and soon their piercing cries were replaced by the sounds of tearing flesh.

Agata's expression returned to normal as the moment of ecstasy passed. She looked melancholy; Leopardo sensed it and kissed her on the back of the head.

'Don't be sad, Mother,' he whispered. 'Less than two days to go now.'

Even though he was used to the goriest sights imaginable, the birdkeeper did not dare look at what had become of the man tied to the post.

Jake was woken by a gentle nudge. He had fallen asleep, as was his wont, amongst the ropes on deck, snugly wrapped in a blanket. Charlie was leaning over him, with Mr Drake peering down from his shoulder.

'I thought you might be interested in something . . .' Charlie whispered (Nathan and Lucius were still sleeping, but Charlie was not so much being polite as enjoying the peace a while longer).

Jake sat up and squinted at the dawn: a band of pink light was emerging above a landmass to their right.

'It's a rather unsettling sight,' Charlie continued, pointing towards a cone-shaped mountain. 'That's Mount Vesuvius there.' His voice became more serious. 'And below it is the town of Pompeii.'

Jake had heard of Pompeii: he knew that it had been destroyed and buried when a huge volcano erupted. He started to make out the shape of a town, high walled and sloping down the hillside between the mountain and the sea. He wasn't sure when exactly Pompeii had met its terrible fate, so he half expected to find it in ruins, but its streets were already busy with early morning activity.

Charlie continued gravely, 'The town has another fifty-two years before calamity strikes. Everything will be wiped out: the forum, the theatres, stadia, temples, shops and palaces, gone in a flash.'

'What happened exactly?' Jake asked, then

corrected himself: 'I mean, what *will* happen?'

'In August AD 79, after eight hundred years of being entirely dormant, that volcano will blow like a volcano has never blown before. A fountain of ash and stone will spew up thousands of metres into the air; it will go on doing so through the day and night. Incredibly, most will survive this, but they'll wish they hadn't. For then will come the pyroclastic event' – Mr Drake edged away from Charlie in distaste; it wasn't so much the words he objected to, rather the florid actions that accompanied them – 'a surge of boiling, choking gas, travelling at two hundred miles an hour, instantly turning everything it touches' – Charlie paused for effect, and snapped his fingers – 'to black carbon.'

Once again Jake scanned the town – the tops of the high city walls were now catching the light of the rising sun – and sadly pondered its fate, taking some comfort from the fact that the people still faced fifty-two years of peace.

'In the other direction' – Charlie pointed far along the coast – 'on that peninsula right at the end of the Bay of Naples, is Misenum, where the Roman fleet is stationed. The Roman navy took a while to get going, but now it is the greatest fleet the world

has ever known. It's quite a sight – have a look.' He retrieved his little telescope, opened it out and handed it to Jake, who trained it on the spur of land far in the distance. At first he couldn't make sense of the puzzle of shapes, but then he saw a succession of wharves, each with a flotilla of vast warships: it looked like a city in its own right.

The quiet of the early morning was broken by Lucius shouting in his sleep: '*Bellum parate! Ferte milites!*' He was lying on his back, his hands twitching as he arrested some imaginary foe. After a couple of minutes of role-play, which included Lucius banging his fists on the deck, Nathan emerged from below in a silk dressing gown, pushing his eye mask up onto his forehead.

'I was hoping *I* was having a bad dream,' he drawled, 'but he's still here.' He went over and prodded Lucius awake with a slippered foot. 'Good morning, Lucy,' he offered with a poisonous smile. 'I'm afraid there are chores to be done. We've drawn lots: you've got latrine cleaning.'

Lucius stared up at him in bemusement.

'For goodness' sake, Nathan,' Charlie grunted with irritation, 'leave him alone. He's done nothing to hurt you.'

But Nathan's expression had changed: he had seen the town of Pompeii across the water. He bowed his head respectfully. 'Poor old place,' he murmured.

A short while later they arrived in the small, neat port of Herculaneum, just up the coast from Pompeii. As Charlie steered the *Conqueror* into the harbour, he explained to Jake that this town would also be destroyed by the volcano, though the damage would not be as bad. Lucius overheard them as he was polishing his sword and asked what they were talking about. Charlie, although he was clearly bending History Keepers' rules about not tampering with the future, told him he didn't think it would be the best place for Lucius to settle down – he was an expert on volcanoes, he explained, and had a bad feeling about this one. Lucius looked at Charlie a little oddly, but Jake got the feeling the Roman would heed the advice nonetheless.

Nathan emerged from below deck and threw a bundle of clothes at Lucius. 'You'd better change,' he told him.

Lucius was still wearing his Hydra uniform. He inspected the offering with a look of contempt.

'And you can take that look off your face. Those are quality garments,' Nathan said, adding under his breath, 'Better than those preposterous outfits *she* makes you wear. Agata's Zeldt's obsession with feathers is lamentable.'

For his own part, Nathan had, rather self-consciously, donned a pair of gladiator's boots and a fitted leather jerkin over his tunic. He collared Jake. 'Now tell me the truth,' he said, striking a pose, 'does this jacket make my arms look bigger?'

'Yes . . .' Jake nodded uncertainly. 'I think so, but it looks a little . . . restricting.' He was right: it was so tight around the tops of his arms, it was impeding the blood flow.

'It's fine.' Nathan gave it a sharp tug. 'What about the boots? They're quite masculine, aren't they?'

'Very manly,' Jake agreed – it seemed the best thing to do.

'Because *he* hasn't got a monopoly on looking like a Roman god.' Nathan gave a jealous nod at Lucius, whose muscles rippled as he changed into his new clothes.

The ship docked and the four of them made their way up the main street towards the theatre, which Charlie had already located on the map.

Jake saw that this was a town with money – it was more prosperous than Messina. The streets here were wide and clean; there was white marble everywhere, and well-dressed groups of people window-shopped, sat by fountains or strolled along the harbour.

'It's really just a holiday town,' Charlie commented. 'Rome on sea, if you like.'

Lucius, for one, was impressed, almost overawed, by the displays of wealth. He blushed when three well-bred young ladies floated by in long silk gowns, fluttering their eyelashes at him.

Nathan watched, agog, but they completely ignored him. 'They obviously didn't see me,' he muttered to Jake. As another two beauties approached, he flexed his muscles and fixed them with his most smouldering stare. But they too only had eyes for Lucius.

'I seem to be invisible!' Nathan complained, tugging again at his jerkin, 'Not even the flicker of a glance in my direction. I mean, really, he's just a meathead, whereas I am brains *and* brawn – all wrapped up in a luxury cloak of sensitivity and *savoir-faire*. What's not to adore?'

At length they came to the theatre, a handsome building with arches around it.

'Obviously it's only nine in the morning,' Charlie pointed out, 'so it's unlikely there'll be anything going on.'

Jake and his companions went through one of the arches into a gloomy atrium that curved around the theatre. From there they followed a winding staircase, emerging into the sunlight of the amphitheatre itself. Jake, Nathan and Charlie took in the scene, entranced.

The open-air auditorium was semicircular, consisting of a curving staircase of stone seats that led down to a raised stage. Behind this was a huge marble wall, fronted by high columns, alcoves and statues; three doorways presumably led backstage. Contrary to Charlie's prediction, there *was* a show going on – a performance by some twenty actors, their faces covered by masks, each with a downturned smile of unhappiness. It was being watched by a smattering of people slouched in the front rows.

'It must be a dress rehearsal.' Charlie gasped in wonder as he soaked up the scene.

Two principal characters, a skinny man and a stout woman, were speaking, while the chorus affected theatrical mimes in response, their body

language altering from despair to anger to horror, and so on.

'They seem to be covering every emotion under the sun,' Nathan giggled. Lucius – the bluff, straight-talking soldier – was the only one who seemed uneasy here: it was all a little too touchy-feely for him.

Suddenly things on stage hotted up, and the stout lady shouted abuse at her skinny companion. Jake and the others assumed that this was part of the play, until the lady threw off her mask, revealing – to Lucius's horror – that she wasn't a lady at all, but a bearded middle-aged man. The actor stamped on his mask and attacked his co-star. The chorus tried to separate them, but the scuffle grew so violent that even the audience was sucked into it. Finally the cross-dressing actor silenced everyone with a parting curse, before storming off, throwing down his wig in disgust.

Jake and Nathan turned to Charlie. 'My Latin is just passable,' Nathan said, 'but I barely caught a word of that.'

Charlie duly translated, explaining – after putting the pieces together – that the man playing the wife was one of two *histriones primi*, or principal

actors. The man who was *supposed* to be playing the husband had left at short notice after some unfortunate business the day before, and the skinny man, the understudy, had taken his place, but was clearly not up to the job. '*Abdico*' was his parting shot: 'I resign.'

'Unfortunate business yesterday?' Jake asked. 'What was that?'

'I don't know exactly,' said Charlie, before adding pointedly, 'But it seems he left with a red-headed woman.' All four of them shared a look. 'Let's go backstage and make further enquiries.'

As the argument onstage continued, Jake and the others crept through one of the doors at the back. They found themselves in a dark passage, full of pieces of scenery, but they could still hear the mutters of the actor. They followed his voice until they reached a dressing room. The man was changing out of his costume, scowling at his reflection in the metal mirror.

Charlie took a deep breath and approached him cautiously, asking in Latin if he might have a word. At first he too received a torrent of abuse, but when he revealed that he and his friends had been watching the dress rehearsal and *totally* sympathized with

the actor's plight, his tone softened. He inclined his head condescendingly and introduced himself as Fico Mirabilis – Fico the Fantastic. There followed another rant – Charlie translated bit by bit, mostly for Jake's benefit – about how impossible it was in this day and age to put on drama of quality in the *Greek* tradition (Fico's eyes moistened at this point); how the spoken word was dead; how the gladiators and the vulgar games in Rome had ruined everything; how it was all about cheap thrills and bums on seats.

Charlie nodded in sympathy (in truth, he was probably the better actor of the two) and waited until Fico had run out of steam, then enquired about the events of the day before. This produced a strange medley of reactions: first anger, then resentment, then deep concern. Jake noticed that, at least twice, he contemptuously spat out the name Agata.

Charlie thanked him, said his goodbyes and turned to the others, smiling. 'I've found out everything we need to know.'

As the four of them headed out onto the street and started making their way back towards the *Conqueror*, Charlie gave a full account. 'Well,' he announced with relish, 'the package that Agata

Zeldt was picking up was not a *thing* – it was a person.'

Jake immediately put two and two together. 'It was the missing actor.'

'Affirmative,' Charlie replied. 'According to Fico, the whole nightmare started months ago when a haughty red-head called Agata Zeldt first swanned into town. She watched a performance and then came backstage afterwards and offered Austerio, who should have been playing the husband, a sum of money to do some *private work* for her. If he agreed, she promised to take him to Rome and make him a star. Neither then nor since has Austerio told his old rival what this secret job was to be.

'Anyway, Agata went off and Fico thought that nothing would come of it. But then, yesterday, she suddenly returned to collect him. Fico was furious, jealous; he thought Austerio was the most dreadful ham and totally undeserving of stardom. However, as they set off, Fico – who is Austerio's oldest friend as well as his most deadly rival – had a dreadful premonition about the whole thing, and is now very worried about him.'

'Well, that's certainly as clear as mud,' Nathan commented. 'Maybe I'm missing something, but

mentoring second-rate actors is not usually the route to world domination.'

'What about Topaz?' Jake asked Charlie. 'Did Fico say she was here as well?'

Charlie stopped and pushed his glasses up his nose. 'Apparently Agata was accompanied only by a fair-haired boy.'

Jake felt another flutter of fear – as did Lucius, who was trailing behind.

'Well, we'd better get on our way,' Jake said. 'We've less than twenty-four hours until we're supposed to meet her.'

The boys hurried back to the *Conqueror* and set sail again, steaming northwards past Misenum and its vast fleet of hulking warships. (Jake counted at least twenty-five docked there, each with a distinctive curling prow, wide striped sails and three rows of oars punctuating their mountainous hulls.) The sun travelled across the sky as they pushed on up the coast, arriving at Ostia late in the afternoon.

'This is as close as we'll get to Rome by ship. It's a further twenty miles across land – which is quite an epic journey in this day and age. I suggest we head for the local forum and seek out transportation there.'

Nathan disembarked. 'Perhaps we could treat

ourselves to a little snack first,' he said, eyeing up a foodstall on the other side of the quay. 'Is that ice cream? Has it been invented yet? We are on the Italian Riviera, after all.'

'Afraid not,' Charlie sighed, jumping ashore along with the others. 'Unless you're an emperor with an army of skivvies to send to the Apennines to collect snow. That I believe is *Pepones et melones* – cold stewed melon with cornstarch. It's perfectly adequate in a pudding emergency' – he shrugged – 'which I actually agree this is.'

Just as they were crossing over to the stall, a horse-drawn cart, laden with all sorts of amphorae, zigzagged out of control along the quayside, nearly running them over before crashing into a low wall. Lucius started berating the ancient driver in no uncertain terms, and a heated discussion ensued; the man's dog joined in, barking and growling in defence of his master. Jake couldn't help but feel a little sorry for the old man: he was so small and frail, and evidently much loved by his more sprightly canine companion.

'Good gracious, is he blind?' Charlie cried suddenly.

Jake looked more closely and realized that he was

right: the man was addressing Lucius as if he were standing somewhere else entirely.

'Now I've seen it all,' Nathan commented. 'Blind cart drivers. The world has gone mad.'

Eventually the cart clattered off into the town and the boys went to buy their melon and corn-starch snack. As Jake ate his (actually, it was more refreshing than it sounded), he eyed up a pair of warships, much like the ones in Misenum, setting sail further up the harbour, their three strict lines of oars beating in unison. Close up, he could see their decks teaming with soldiers and wondered on what mission, to what part of the huge Roman Empire, they were departing.

'Being so close to Rome,' Charlie explained, 'there's a strong military presence here too.' He thought about it. 'In fact, let's face it, there's a military presence everywhere.'

Suddenly Mr Drake started shaking in panic.

'What's up?' Charlie asked.

'I can see what's up,' Jake gasped, his eyes fixed on a group of figures coming along the harbour towards them, clad in grey leather breastplates with feathered shoulders and beaked bronze masks.

'Hydra!' exclaimed Nathan. 'They must have

followed us here. How did we not see them?'

Just then there was a sharp *thwack!* and a metal dart struck Nathan's *Pepones et melones*, sending it splattering all over him. 'Now that is just rude,' he snapped, then grimaced as he saw four more guards approaching from the other direction. 'Heads!' he shouted as another volley of arrows flew through the air. Some locals ran for cover, while Mr Drake, now in a complete flutter, ducked under Charlie's toga.

'Up here!' Charlie commanded, leading them away from the port, for there was no way to reach their ship without meeting the enemy. As they hurried on, the whole retinue of guards were soon in pursuit.

'Over there! Quickly!' Nathan yelled, rushing towards a large porticoed building on one side of the street. They flew across the marble atrium and through a set of double doors. Nathan caught his leather jerkin on the handle, lost his balance and careered spectacularly across the wet marble floor.

'Damn this thing!' he cursed as he finally straightened up – to see forty pairs of disapproving eyes trained on him. There were men everywhere, mostly old, either swimming or lounging by the giant pool that dominated the room, most of them

stark naked. 'Ah, the public baths,' Nathan mumbled with an apologetic bow. 'I'd forgotten how they like to put it all on show.' Quickly and carefully, his eyes trained on the floor, he followed the others out of the chamber.

Behind them, the doors flew open again, and six soldiers rushed in, drawing their swords. The bathers gasped and backed away or sank into the pool as the guards advanced on the History Keepers.

'Swords?' Nathan grinned. 'That's a little more sportsmanlike.' He drew his own, and Charlie and Jake quickly followed suit.

Lucius was shaking his head. 'You not fight close: they have poison on the arm – it puts you to sleep.'

Nathan and Jake didn't have a clue what he was talking about, but Charlie saw that each guard had a silver device strapped to his forearm. 'I think he's saying that those bracelets contain some sort of tranquillizer.'

'How perfectly charming,' Nathan drawled. 'They weren't wearing them before?'

'Not at camp,' Lucius explained, 'but always outside.'

'It's a shame you didn't have time to pick up

yours.' Nathan nodded at Lucius's bare wrist.

They turned and ran through an archway and down a passage. The soldiers dashed after them, pushing a group of cowering bathers into the pool.

Jake, Lucius, Nathan and Charlie flew into the *palaestra* – the gymnasium – where athletes were training with weights and stretching equipment. 'Excuse us,' said Jake, politely taking a small lead dumb-bell from a man with pumped-up muscles and an attitude to match, and pitching it towards the doorway. The others followed his example, grabbing whatever missiles they could find – leather balls stuffed with sand, iron discuses; even the stone busts from a series of alcoves – and hurling them across the room. Some hit their targets before crashing to the ground, but mostly the barrage of projectiles bounced harmlessly off the marble floor.

Negotiating the maze of corridors, they finally saw another set of doors ahead of them. As they ran towards them, a matronly woman in a white veil tried to stop them. '*Vires interdicti sunt!*' she cried as they swept past her.

'What's she saying?' Jake asked.

'Men forbidden,' replied Charlie with a shrug.

They opened the doors and went in, immediately

235

aware of streams of incense wafting up from two golden braziers. A young girl strummed a lyre as five women of various ages lay on wooden tables to receive a massage. They turned in alarm as the intruders shattered the peace.

'Ladies – or should I say *goddesses*?' Nathan said roguishly, catching the eye of a pretty masseuse.

Charlie rolled his eyes at Jake as Nathan took the jar from her and sniffed its contents. 'Lavender and neroli – there's nothing better for balanced skin and a radiant glow,' he commented before flinging the oil across the shiny floor in front of the doorway.

It was a masterstroke: as the soldiers burst in, they lost their footing, skidding in all directions. Nathan completed the move by upturning one of the incense braziers and igniting the oil, which set fire to the feathered boots of three of the guards.

'Thank you.' Nathan winked at his goddess, who seemed terrified and intrigued in equal measure. 'I've been suffering from a crisis of confidence – but I can see from your face that I still have what it takes.'

'Where does he get these awful lines?' Charlie asked the others. No one replied as they hurried along more white marble passages until they reached a wide atrium.

'Up there!' shouted Charlie. He was pointing to a large open window, at head height, overlooking the garden. Lucius clasped his hands together and gave him a leg up. Nathan did the same for Jake. Charlie jumped down the other side, but Jake waited as Lucius offered to help Nathan.

'After you,' the latter replied smugly. Lucius, in another of his gravity-defying leaps, was up and over the wall in a flash. Nathan tried to improve on it, but his hand – still drenched in lavender oil – slipped, and he fell back down, hitting his head on the ledge and twisting his ankle as he landed on the floor. Jake could see that the two remaining guards were coming up the corridor, preceded by their long shadows.

'Here!' shouted Jake, leaning down, his hand held out. But Nathan was still dazed from his fall, and looked up blearily at Jake, only half recognizing him. 'Nathan!' Jake shouted again.

The American turned to look around the room, an expression of wonder on his face. 'Have I got a massage booked? Aromatherapy?'

There was nothing for it: 'Wait for us!' Jake shouted at the others as he jumped down and grabbed his friend. 'Nathan!' he shouted again, this

time slapping his face. It had the desired effect: Nathan's eyes came back into focus – as did his instinct for survival. There was no time to reach the window, so Jake pulled him down one of the four passageways that led out of the atrium. The two soldiers followed, now hard on their heels.

Ahead of them was a single door; wisps of hot steam escaped from all around it. Jake pulled it open and they found themselves in a large, vaulted chamber that was thick with vapour.

The heat was tremendous and Jake could feel his lungs contract. As they edged forward into the steam, they could see the shapes of bathers.

The door creaked open behind them to let in a wedge of light and two brutish figures; then the light was gone again. Two shadows advanced, swords held out before them.

'Any ideas?' Nathan whispered to Jake as they retreated to the back wall.

Jake looked around. He could just make out three vents in the floor, with hot air billowing out of them. He recalled how once, during the school holidays, he had helped his dad fit a steam room in the house of a film director (Alan had boasted that this was the start of the big time, but of course it

238

had all ended in humiliating disaster and threats of a lawsuit). But Jake remembered how dangerous steam could be if pressurized.

'Move that onto the last vent,' he instructed Nathan, indicating a trough of water. Nathan did as he was told, while Jake did the same with the first vent. 'Now give me your jacket.'

'What?' Nathan replied. 'My gladiator's jerkin?'

'Just give it to me – you hate it anyway.'

Nathan reluctantly took it off and handed it over. Jake placed it on top of the central vent. Now, with all three openings sealed, the chamber started to empty of steam surprisingly quickly, and the two guards were suddenly visible.

'Here!' Jake called over to them, holding up his sword. The soldiers muttered something to each other and came in for the kill. 'When I give the word,' Jake whispered to Nathan, 'pull the jacket out of the way.' He waited, his sword clutched firmly in his hand. The men approached, the sharp edges of their swords glinting in the half-light.

'Now!' he shouted. Nathan quickly drew the jacket aside and a jet of boiling steam surged up into the soldiers' faces, burning and blinding them.

As Jake and Nathan made a dash for the door,

one of the guards fumbled for Jake's arm, but he pulled away, kicking his assailant on the knee and sending him sprawling. However, as he collapsed, the guard managed to twist open the capsule on his silver bracelet. A tiny cloud of noxious vapour was released. It had the stench of putrefying flesh – just like the corpse flowers in the laboratory in Vulcano. It made Jake gag immediately; his nose burned and his throat seized up. Then his vision blurred and darkened; it was as if his brain was shutting down. He felt his strength draining away and fell, before Nathan caught him and dragged him out of the room.

The next few minutes were like a bad dream. Jake was half aware of stumbling along more passageways and finally out into the sunlight again. There was running and shouting. Charlie and Lucius came briefly into focus, along with Mr Drake, and Jake was bundled onto the back of a cart. He was moving – then he heard more shouting; finally the confusion of faces and noises dissolved and he blacked out completely.

13 TO THE ETERNAL CITY

Jake awoke to some exquisite aromas. Although his head throbbed and he could still taste the Hydra's poison (much like the after-effects of being drugged in London when he had first met Jupitus Cole), a fragrance like rose petals revived his spirits immediately.

He opened his bleary eyes to find himself in the back of a cart, rattling across the countryside of Latium as the sun was starting to set. Lucius was snoozing by his side and Nathan was staring at the road ahead. They were surrounded by terracotta jars that looked somehow familiar – and were the source of the delicious scent.

'Feeling all right?' Nathan asked, on seeing him stir.

Jake nodded, though in truth he still felt nauseous and groggy.

'That's quite some soporific they let off,' Nathan commented, passing Jake a beaker of water. 'I almost blacked out too. The guards must be resistant to it.'

Jake took a long cool sip. He was about to ask where they were and how they had got onto the cart when a dog leaped down from the driver's seat and started licking his face. Jake recognized it immediately: it was the faithful hound of the old blind man who had nearly run them over in Ostia. Jake put two and two together. He turned round to find that very same man sitting at the front of the cart, chatting and laughing, Charlie at his side with the reins in his hand. Pulling them along was a sturdy horse who looked every bit as friendly as the dog. Mr Drake sat contentedly on his master's shoulder, inspecting the darkening countryside.

'Charlie did a deal,' Nathan explained. '*We* get a lift to Rome; old Gaius there gets to be driven without crashing into everything coming the other way.' Jake looked over at the man's kind face, crinkled brown by decades in the Italian sun. 'He has a story that even I found quite moving,' Nathan continued, putting his hand to his heart (though, as usual, it was the wrong side). 'He comes from a small town

on the coast south of Ostia, and used to be a carpenter – built boats, houses, everything. Then he suffered a string of disasters: first his wife became ill – she's still stuck in bed – and then he went blind. How's that for luck? He couldn't work any more, because he couldn't see, but he could smell. So he took to making perfumes, distilling them from the wild flowers of the region. The idea was to sell them to the baths there in Ostia, but the snooty manager tried to fleece him – which makes me feel less guilty about the state we left it in – so he decided to head for the markets of the Eternal City.' He shook his mane of hair and smiled winningly. 'That's Rome, by the way.'

'What happened to the *Conqueror*?' Jake asked.

'We weren't able to get back to check on it,' Nathan replied. 'It had been commandeered by our pursuers – we seem to have eluded them by the way, but keep an eye out just in case. We'll have to keep our fingers crossed that the ancient Rome bureau is still in one piece and there's a Meslith machine there – otherwise we're completely in the dark. Anyway, make yourself comfortable: we'll be travelling through the night.'

Jake looked at Gaius's dog, who was now lying

with his head on Lucius's chest, blinking happily. He realized how much he missed Felson, even though they had only known each other for a matter of weeks.

Jake's thoughts turned to his parents and he wondered how they were getting on with the unfathomable Oceane Noire.

Finally he wondered about Topaz; he prayed that they would find her. Would she make the appointment on the Pons Fabricius; and if so, what state would she be in . . . ? A host of dark thoughts began to gather in his mind. He decided to stop thinking until they reached Rome.

'Rome . . .' he murmured. 'I'm going to ancient Rome.' Now tantalizingly close, the immensity of the idea dawned on him. To visit the city; to see its great buildings intact; to walk amongst its people; to visit the most famous civilization of all time . . . it was a thing of true wonder.

The cart rattled its way up a slope and down into an immense valley, stretching out for miles and miles ahead of them. The road cut a perfectly straight line across it.

They travelled into the night, Charlie, Nathan and Jake taking it in turns at the reins. The song of

a million cicadas, hidden amongst the wild flowers of the roadside, floated on the warm air, and a bright three-quarter moon rose in the sky. At the halfway point they stopped for water and refreshments. They changed horses (Charlie negotiated a deal with a yawning innkeeper: Gaius would pick up his own nag – to which he was much attached – on his return), filled the lanterns with oil and set off again. There was still some distance to go and they couldn't risk missing their rendezvous with Topaz.

Occasionally they met another vehicle travelling in the other direction. The twinkling lights seemed to take an eternity to reach them, but finally the oncoming cart would rattle past. As Jake was dozing off, one of these caught his attention. He heard a distinctive clink well before it drew level with them. The driver was dressed in Moorish clothes, and when Jake gave him a tentative smile, he stared back with dark eyes from under his hood – before saluting him with a warm nod; just a stranger from another time, saying hello. His load consisted of stacks of silver, copper and pewter – plates, cups and trinkets – that glinted in the moonlight. The sight of this ancient treasure trove disappearing off into the night added to the sheer magic of the evening.

*   *   *

'I bought shellfish!' Rose announced, shutting the door with her sandaled foot and heading into the garden. 'Oh! Good gracious . . .' She did a double-take when she saw the constellation of pretty lights – hundreds of candles and lamps – illuminating the terraces.

She called out, 'I didn't intend to buy crab – not live crab, in any case' – she looked uncertainly down at something twitching in her basket – 'but I'm afraid my Latin is on the rusty side. Jupitus, are you there?'

He identified himself by languorously raising an arm in the twinkling gloom. 'Lovely lights,' Rose cooed, bustling over to his seat overlooking the bay. 'Are we celebrating something?'

'Not at all,' Jupitus replied acidly. 'I just need to see where I'm going. Unless you would like me to break my other leg?'

'And demand twice the amount of sympathy?' Rose giggled. 'I don't think I have it in me. Now,' she said, cautiously reaching into her basket, 'as you know, I'm not frightened of many things, but I find live crustaceans a challenge at the best of times— Ow!' She yanked her arm back as a giant

246

crab shot out and landed on Jupitus's chest.

'Off, off!' he yelled in fury as it fell onto his lap. He swiped it aside with the back of his hand. It quickly righted itself and went scurrying away across the terrace.

'No, no!' Rose went chasing after it as it zigzagged this way and that.

Jupitus watched, at first with deep irritation, then with growing amusement as Rose kept closing in on it, then shrieking as it defended itself with its pincers and took off once more. By the time it had taken refuge in a pool of water below a fountain, Jupitus was laughing so hard that his stomach hurt.

'Let the poor thing be,' he called out to Rose. 'I think it's earned its freedom – if only for cheering me up.'

'Jupitus Cole, you really are infuriating some- times!' Rose retorted, storming back towards him. 'You're a miserable, mean-spirited piece of work. Look!' She held up her hands, which were covered in cuts. 'Anyway, it serves you right – they'll be no dinner now.'

'No dinner?' said Jupitus in distress.

'No. And no bedtime story either!'

'Well, just as well there's a plan B,' Jupitus replied

in his most velvety tones, and pointed towards a table (Rose had not noticed it tucked underneath the vast bougainvillea) that was laid out with the most magnificent banquet: grilled fish, fresh salads and platters of cold meats. Not only did the food look delicious, but the presentation, gleaming cutlery, and flowers and candles, was stunning.

Rose's anger melted away. 'How on earth did you manage to do all that?'

'Not bad for a miserable mean-spirited piece of work?' he said with a twinkle in his eye.

At that moment the Meslith machine, which was sitting on a side table, started to come alive, its crystalline rod fizzing with electricity. The smile left Jupitus's face immediately. 'Not again,' he sighed to himself.

'Who is it?' Rose asked.

'My darling fiancée, no doubt,' he replied through gritted teeth.

'Well, it must be important,' said Rose, advancing to look.

'Leave it!' Jupitus snapped, then softened. 'Please.' He took the blanket from under his leg and chucked it over the machine. Then he turned to

Rose and, smiling again, motioned for her to sit. 'Let's enjoy our dinner . . .'

In another corner of Europe, a thousand miles and many more years away from Messina, Alan was standing guard at the entrance to Oceane Noire's suite. He had one eye on the candlelit corridor and staircase and the other on Miriam, who was snooping around inside with a lamp. 'Can you find anything at all?' he called in a loud whisper.

'Nothing yet . . .' Miriam called back. 'Just lots of rather dramatic paintings of her majesty.' She gave a giggle.

They were following their son's advice and searching Oceane's quarters for any sign of treachery – in particular, a book with a picture of a palm tree; the one she was carrying the night Jake discovered her in the archives.

Miriam gazed around at the large and opulent space, fitted out in the style of Versailles before the French Revolution. There were plush chaise longues, elegant screens and gilt-edged tables. Adorning the silk-lined walls were portraits of Oceane in different 'romantic' costumes: as a Grecian deity, an Egyptian queen, a Turkish flower

seller, and so on. Miriam struggled to focus on the job in hand.

One painting, however, she simply could not pass by without greater scrutiny. 'Oceane Noire, you are ridiculous,' she snorted to herself as she held her lamp up to it. Here, Oceane was depicted as a mysterious eastern princess surrounded by palms and palaces, lording it over a handsome gardener – who was clearly a less pale, more virile version of Jupitus Cole.

'Someone's coming!' Alan suddenly called from the doorway.

Miriam swung round and, in her panic, knocked the painting sideways. As she was about to straighten it, she noticed something hidden behind. She carefully slid the picture further to one side, revealing a small door. There was a lock with a little key in it. Miriam turned it, opened the door and saw a tiny secret compartment lined with purple velvet. It was completely empty. She hurriedly shut the door and covered her tracks.

'Too late! She's here!' Alan whimpered in desperation. From the doorway he could see Oceane's shadow quickly ascending the staircase. 'You'll have to hide,' he called over, before retreating

quickly down the passageway in the opposite direction. He had just managed to slip into the shadows when Oceane appeared at the top of the stairs, pulling Josephine along behind her. Her skirts flared out on either side as she strode into her suite and slammed the door shut behind her. She was too wrapped up in herself to notice Miriam disappear behind one of the folding screens.

Miriam watched as Oceane went over to the portrait and opened the secret compartment. From a pocket in her dress she produced a book – on which Miriam identified a palm tree – placed it inside, closed the door, locked it and threw the key into a pink china pot (also decorated with her likeness) on the mantelshelf. Finally she carefully repositioned the painting.

Meanwhile Miriam watched, aghast, as Josephine padded straight towards the screen.

There was a soft knock on the door. 'Mademoiselle Noire, might I have a quick word?' It was Alan's voice.

'*Qu'est-ce que vous voulez?*' she spat when she found him outside, a rigid smile on his face.

'There seems to be water leaking downstairs,' he said sheepishly. 'Might I check your bathroom?'

Oceane grimaced in irritation. 'I have the worst headache known to mankind. *Depêchez-vous!*'

'If you could just show me where it is,' Alan replied loudly, for Miriam's benefit.

Oceane grunted and led him across the room. Now Miriam made a dash for the door, only to hear a full-throated roar behind her. 'Just shut up, you imbecile lion,' Oceane cursed, silencing her pet immediately. As she disappeared into the next room, Miriam finally managed to slip out and close the door behind her.

Ten minutes later, safely back in their own cosy room, Alan and Miriam, breathless and excited, started to ponder how and when they might get their hands on the book with the palm tree on it and discover what significance it had.

Just before dawn, the traffic began to increase. Soon other roads converged with theirs, forming a wide thoroughfare. Traders and farmers jostled with private carts and carriages. Nathan had the reins and Charlie was describing all the sights to an enthralled Gaius. Jake sat up, excited at the prospect of seeing the ancient city. Even Lucius awoke from his long sleep and took in the sights while stretching his bulky frame.

But this last section of the journey soon grew frustrating: after a series of hold-ups, the traffic finally stopped completely. A huge load of marble had been shed in an impossibly narrow stretch of road, and it took nearly two hours to shift it – and calm the fight that flared up when, for a moment, swords were drawn. It was well past eight by the time the way was cleared, and Jake feared that they might miss Topaz.

Gradually buildings started to materialize out of the dust and heat – just clusters to begin with, but soon becoming more densely packed.

As they passed a line of stalls selling cheap food and household items, Lucius suddenly stood up. 'Do you have money?' he asked Nathan, pointing to one of the stalls. Nathan suspiciously withdrew his pouch. Lucius snatched a copper coin, jumped down and purchased a jar, before leaping aboard the moving cart again.

'Don't mention it,' said Nathan sarcastically.

As the cart trundled on, Lucius popped the cork and took a slug of the contents, grimacing, then passed it to Nathan. 'You need to drink. All of you.'

'What is it?' the American drawled.

'Vinegar.'

Nathan pushed it away politely. 'Thanks all the same, but I'm not thirsty.' He pulled a face at the others. 'He is actually unsound of mind.'

'Drink,' Lucius insisted. 'It will stop poison from Hydra. You all drink. We soldiers, we drink in case of accident.'

Charlie cottoned on at once. 'I think he means it's a kind of vaccine for that gas. I suppose we'd better do as he says.' He grabbed the flask and took a big sip.

Reluctantly Nathan and Jake did the same. Jake didn't like vinegar at the best of times and struggled to keep the sharp, acrid stuff down.

'It good maybe three hours,' Lucius explained. 'Then you must drink again. This will keep you safe.'

'I love this job sometimes,' said Nathan drily as they rattled on through the suburbs.

As he looked around, Jake couldn't help feeling a little sorry for the people who lived here: the houses were misshapen tenement blocks, four or five tottering storeys high and packed one next to the other with narrow dark passageways between. From a window Jake noticed a thin arm empty a chamber pot onto the grimy street below. There were

red-faced drunks sleeping in doorways, thin cats and dogs searching for a meal amongst the waste. Pungent smells – of decaying food, of sweat and urine – floated across the hot air. It was not quite the Rome that Jake had imagined.

Charlie sensed his disappointment. 'Just wait till we've climbed the pass between the Caelian and Aventine hills,' he said, pointing to the slope ahead of them. 'It will be another world.'

He was not exaggerating. Five minutes later the road levelled out and ancient Rome spread out before them.

Jake's eyes widened; his jaw dropped; he gaped in wonder. Lucius did the same. Even Nathan was struck dumb. Charlie smiled with the satisfaction of someone who has just magicked from thin air something truly sensational.

Ahead of them, occupying a huge area between seven undulating hills, was a limitless collection of temples, squares and arenas; mile upon mile of brilliant white marble that shimmered in the morning sun. Grand villas spilled down the sides of the hills, and the elegant streets were teeming with life.

'That, if I am not mistaken,' Charlie declared, a tear coming to his eye, 'is the capital city of a

civilization that will change the world for ever. The first truly global metropolis. The Romans did so much for history, it's easy to take them for granted.'

'He's right of course,' Nathan concurred, 'although when I try and remember *what* they invented, I always go slightly blank.' He added mischievously, 'I know they were responsible for some shocking haircuts. And curling tongs.'

Charlie became quite flustered and started counting things off on his hand. 'Well, let's see . . . they were pioneers of education, architecture, sanitation, irrigation and modern government. They revolutionized road building, town planning and law.'

'Yes, but apart from that . . .' Nathan winked at Jake.

'They brought us our language, our alphabet, the police system, the benefit system, the sewage system; water-powered milling, high-rise buildings, the calendar, paved streets, glassed windows, public libraries, cement; even apples and pears!' Charlie had started to go red. 'And yes, eventually the Roman Empire crumbled – but their legacy lives on, Nathan Wylder, in every corner of this planet up to Point Zero and beyond.'

'I'm pulling your leg, Charlie,' Nathan chuckled. 'I love Rome just as much as you. Look at it. It's the opposite of shy and retiring. It's got real guts.'

'What's that?' said Jake, pointing down towards a gigantic structure in the basin below them. He felt he should change the subject before the argument got any more heated. A stadium, almost half a mile long, bordered by banks of stone seats, was set within a rectangular colonnade of mind-blowing proportions.

Now it was Nathan's turn to show excitement. 'I've only ever seen it in books. Or as ruins. That,' he announced, 'is the Circus Maximus.'

'*That's* the Circus Maximus?' Lucius repeated in awe. 'It's beautiful.'

'The biggest stadium ever built,' Nathan exclaimed, 'accommodating a staggering hundred and fifty thousand spectators. Obviously it's most famous for its chariot racing, but all sorts of things go on there: gladiatorial contests, grand processions, athletics tournaments and spectacular hunts. Signor Gondolfino tells a really gory story of how he watched sixty-three leopards and eighty-nine wild bears being brought down before his very eyes.'

'With all due respect,' Charlie interrupted

irritably (he detested cruelty to animals), 'the signore does like to exaggerate. Anyway, we're running out of time. The Pons Fabricius is over there' – he pointed – 'running from the city to the Tiber Island. I suggest we hurry up.'

It was only a few minutes before nine, and the bridge was still some way off. Jake could see it in the distant haze: just north of the Circus Maximus, where the river curved round in a loop, it crossed over to an island in the middle. A second bridge, identical in design, ran from the island to the fields on the west bank. Nathan urged the horse on, and the cart rattled down into the pulsing city.

The noise was overwhelming: the din of hooves, the clatter of wheels and the frantic buzz of a million inhabitants. There were so many sights that Jake didn't know where to turn first. People bustled about in every direction: workmen gathered up their tools and started their jobs; groups of children in neat togas were marched to school; ladies strolled under the shade of parasols; soldiers in chain mail swaggered out of their barracks. Animals of all sorts joined the throng: herds of sheep and cows were driven to market; mules and donkeys carried great baskets of goods; dogs of every shape and size played

in the streets, padded along with their masters or watched, yawning, from shady doorways.

Mostly the people were dressed in rough, simple clothes, but occasionally important-looking figures in brilliant white togas would forge their way through the rabble. One of these, Jake observed, had a toga fringed with a band of deep purple. He was surrounded by armoured bodyguards who were roughly pushing people out of his way. Following him was a trail of hangers-on, all competing for his attention.

Some people didn't travel on foot at all, but were carried in cushioned litters, veiled from the hubbub by swags of silk. Jake spotted a pale-faced, thin-lipped woman thrust her head through the curtains and bark orders to her bearers, even giving one a lash of her whip.

The streets were lined with shops of every kind. They were open-fronted, windowless, and most had rough counters and painted signs to show what they were selling. There were blacksmiths, goldsmiths, stone cutters and carpenters; florists, bakers, fruiterers and honey-sellers; there was an apothecary, where a pharmacist was pounding herbs with a pestle and mortar; and a copy shop where three hunched

scribes carefully duplicated documents onto scrolls of parchment; there were sandal makers, lamp makers, locksmiths and potters; Jake noticed that there were even barbers and hairdressers.

One such place caught his eye: in a gaudy salon with painted walls and garlands of flowers, a number of ladies were having their hair done and ointments applied to their faces. One was telling a story in dramatic hushed tones while the others hung on her every word. The whole scene made Jake think that very little had changed since AD 27.

Nathan urged the horse through the maze of streets. But as their way became increasingly narrow and densely packed, Jake suggested that it would be quicker to continue on foot. Nine a.m. had already come and gone, and he was feeling quite frantic. The others agreed. To say thank you to old Gaius, Charlie offered to help him set up his stall in the Forum Boarium; he would meet the others on the bridge presently.

Jake, Nathan and Lucius quickly said their good-byes, hugging the old man, then set off, weaving their way purposefully through the teeming crowd. Jake's heart was thumping again: if all went according to plan, he would be face to face with

Topaz in a matter of minutes. The sense of anticipation was both joyful and painful. Faster and faster they ran, until eventually they emerged through the old city gates and found themselves on the banks of the Tiber.

'There!' Jake shouted, pointing towards the bridge that crossed over to the island. He took the lead, breaking into a run again.

'Slow down, Jake,' Nathan ordered. 'We need to keep our wits about us. There's always the chance we're walking into a trap.'

Jake reluctantly obeyed. At length they were striding onto the Pons Fabricius, heads swivelling, alert for danger. People were walking briskly to and fro, or milling about chatting, or watching the jugglers, fire eaters and fortune tellers. Jake eagerly scanned the figures and finally spied a young woman: she was leaning over the parapet, her back to them, gazing down at the river. She wore a hooded gown, as delicate as gossamer, from which strayed locks of honey-coloured hair. Jake could contain himself no longer: he rushed over, eyes wide, breath fast, mouth dry.

'Topaz?'

The girl turned round and Jake's heart sank: it

was not her. She was about the same age but her features were plain and she had none of Topaz's mystery. Jake smiled, embarrassed, and turned away. Catching up, Nathan shot him a reproachful look, but Jake was too preoccupied to notice, turning to examine the other people on the bridge.

He soon realized that there was no one else even remotely like Topaz St Honoré.

The three of them waited, leaning against the balustrade, eagerly straightening up whenever they spotted a female figure. After an hour their spirits began to sink. Jake maintained a forced smile, but his eyes were sad.

There was a brief respite when Charlie arrived bearing drinks, snacks and a cheerful account of how Gaius's perfumes were already creating a stir in the marketplace. He then clapped eyes on Tiber Island and became very excited. He told them the legend of how it was formed. 'Five hundred years ago, the body of the last king of Rome, Tarquinius Superbus, a terrible despot, was thrown into the river. Gradually all the mud and silt built up around him until it formed an island. And have you noticed,' he asked, 'that it is now shaped like a boat?'

Lucius looked at Charlie as if he was mad, but

Jake immediately saw the resemblance. The front of the island narrowed sharply like a prow, at its centre a great obelisk shot up like a mast, and a temple set amongst the trees at the rear was the high stern.

'Of course, that is no coincidence,' Charlie went on.

'Goes without saying – that would be idiotic,' Nathan muttered under his breath.

'No indeed – the rulers of Rome wanted it to look like a ship in honour of Aesculapius, the Greek god of healing. You see, three hundred-odd years ago, in 293 BC, there was a dreadful plague, and an envoy was sent to Greece, to the god's spiritual home. As was the custom, a special snake was brought back from there. It spent the return journey wrapped tightly around the mast of the ship. However, when they sailed up the Tiber, it suddenly leaped overboard and slithered across to the island, showing that this was where the temple should be built. And there it stands to this day – Rome's very own shrine to Aesculapius' – he trembled at the sheer poetry of the story – 'on a ship-shaped island!'

'Fascinating!' Nathan murmured through slightly gritted teeth. 'Sometimes I think your talents are wasted on us. Perhaps you should give tours to the locals?'

Charlie just rolled his eyes and shoved his glasses up his nose, muttering something about philistines.

As the sun reached its zenith and the heat became unbearable, Nathan decided he no longer cared what he looked like and bought a parasol – a pink lady's one with tassels, which was the only one left. He put it up and twirled it with such panache, he managed to get away with it.

By mid-afternoon there was still no sign of Topaz. Jake sat morosely, barely moving a muscle, his hopeful smile long gone. The others became fidgety. Lucius went to have his fortune told and objected when the clairvoyant insisted he was destined to be a sheep farmer in Germania. Meanwhile Nathan, to take his mind off things, decided to get his portrait painted by a local artist with a face like a squeezed lemon, who clearly felt that such work was beneath him. Needless to say, Nathan was the customer from hell, insisting in his pigeon Latin that the man had failed to catch his *true manly mystique*. A hushed row ensued, with the artist finally tossing the picture into the Tiber. 'Romans are just *so* touchy,' Nathan complained as Charlie came to calm things down.

The afternoon turned to evening. One by one

the entertainers packed up and left, and the traffic across the bridge slowed to a trickle. As darkness fell about them, and the city dissolved into a myriad of twinkling lights, Charlie took a deep breath and finally voiced the fears of all.

'She's obviously not coming. I suggest we make our way to the bureau. She might contact us there, or we may get word from Point Zero. At least we can find Agata Zeldt's location in Rome. Does everyone agree?'

Nathan and Lucius reluctantly pulled themselves to their feet, but Jake did not move. 'I'll stay here,' he muttered.

'Probably not such a good idea,' Nathan said quietly. 'This place is dangerous at night. The whole city is. The bandits come out like vampires.'

Jake shrugged. 'I think you should go and find the bureau, but I want to stay here.'

Nathan and Charlie exchanged a look.

'I stay with him,' said Lucius, puffing out his chest. 'I am not frightened of bandits. I eat them for breakfast. Go! Yake and I stay together.'

For a moment Jake thought he would rather take his chances with bandits than with Lucius, but then he smiled up at him. Nathan and Charlie took some

convincing, but in the end it seemed sensible to split up. Nathan even grudgingly agreed that Lucius, for all his faults, was the strongest of the four and most suited to the job. They agreed to meet again the following morning, and Nathan and Charlie set off for the bureau.

To begin with Jake and Lucius sat quietly, only occasionally smiling at each other or commenting on the weather (a chill wind had drifted up the river, banishing the day's heat). Then Lucius offered to show off his repertoire of bird songs. Jake listened to them one by one, and although he thought they all sounded the same, his nods of appreciation encouraged Lucius to continue for an hour. Occasionally they heard hurried footsteps approaching in the darkness. They would both look up, reaching for their swords, but there was no sign of Topaz. Silence would fall again, punctuated only by dogs howling from nearby streets or distant bells tolling.

By the middle of the night, both were feeling cold and miserable. To take his mind off things, Jake decided to find out some more about his companion: 'So, did you always want to be a soldier?' He knew it was a silly question.

There was a long pause and Lucius's eyes narrowed. 'No,' he replied brusquely. There was another lengthy silence, then he added, 'My father was a shipbuilder in Apulia. I thought I would do the same.'

'Ships – really? That's amazing.' Jake was certain he had found a good subject.

'Amazing?' his companion grunted sarcastically. 'Really? You know nothing.'

Jake was taken aback – even in the gloom, he could see the sudden murderous look on Lucius's face. There was another hiatus before he continued delicately, 'And your father? Is he still . . .?'

'Not seen my father in seven years,' Lucius snapped. 'Or my mother.' He didn't look at Jake, but seemed fascinated by something on the back of his hand.

It was clearly a sore point. 'Sorry, I didn't mean to . . .' Jake's voice trailed off, but then he went on quietly, 'I know how you feel. I lost my—'

Lucius interrupted Jake with even more venom: 'We change subject – yes?' To show that the matter was closed, he stood up, tugged at his tunic and strode over to the other side of the bridge, his lips pursed.

Jake yearned to talk to him; to tell him how he too had lost his parents for a while. The story of how he found them again might reassure Lucius. Jake also longed to share his own heartache for his lost brother. On the other hand, he was hurt by Lucius's reaction; it was as if he were the only person in the world who had ever suffered.

Conversation stalled after that. They were both exhausted and tetchy. Jake pulled his cloak around him and settled down beside the stone balustrade; and just as he was thinking it would be impossible even to doze in such a place, he drifted off.

14 Dawn Encounter

Jake woke to the sound of footsteps. He sat up. His neck was stiff and his throat parched. Dawn was breaking across the city, and shafts of searing light extended between the buildings. They burned into his eyes, making it almost impossible to see the lone armour-clad figure heading from the city gates towards the bridge – a slight figure, walking with a determined stride.

'Lucius,' Jake called over to his companion.

In a flash the soldier's eyes were open, and he fixed them on the approaching form. A moment later, he was on his feet, his sword drawn.

When Jake realized that the figure wore the feathered epaulets and helmet of the Hydra, he too hurriedly unsheathed his weapon. 'What do we do? Do we run?' he asked, looking around for the best escape route.

'Two of us, one of him,' Lucius grunted, clutching his sword tightly while grabbing the jar of vinegar, pulling the cork out with his teeth and taking a swig. He passed it to Jake, who followed suit. He could see something bulging on the forearm of the advancing man – presumably a metal bracelet. Jake wasn't sure about Lucius's plan of action – more soldiers could well be approaching from different directions. He peered over the parapet to see if they could escape by water, but below them – a long way down – surged a foamy torrent.

The man did not break stride, his boots echoing on the stone bridge, his helmet glinting in the morning sun.

'Hold your ground,' Lucius growled at Jake, feet planted, ready to rebuff an attack. The man continued to advance. Jake stood beside Lucius, narrowed his eyes, and assumed a warlike stance.

The man stopped just short of them. For a moment he did not move. All three of them stood there like statues at the midpoint of the bridge. There was silence, broken only by a flock of lapwings taking flight over the island.

Jake realized that the metal bulge around the

stranger's forearm was not a device, but a tightly wrapped length of thick chain. The man removed his helmet. Immediately long honey-coloured tresses tumbled down. There was a moment of astonished silence, then Jake's face lit up.

'Topaz!' he exclaimed, his heart soaring.

'*Je savais que tu attendrais*. I knew you would wait,' she replied breathlessly, rushing towards him and hugging him tight. 'It's so good to see you. I didn't know who to expect. Sorry I am so late. I could not get away.' As she clung onto him, Topaz and Lucius shared a lingering look.

Jake blushed. 'Yes, well,' he said in the deepest voice he could muster, 'Nathan and Charlie are here too. They went to find the bureau.' He could hardly get the words out; he was so overwhelmed by the warmth of Topaz's welcome, especially after the coolness of their last meeting aboard the *Lindwurm*. He noted that she had come straight to him, not Lucius, and suddenly felt thrilled.

However, now Topaz broke away and turned to the soldier. 'You know, the last time I saw Jake,' she said, 'he sailed all the way up the Rhine just to save me; fought his way onto the enemy's ship. *C'est le garçon le plus courageux que je connais*. He's the

bravest boy I know,' she said, tickling him under the chin, 'and he's even more adorable when he blushes like that.'

Jake went a deeper shade of crimson as Lucius took Topaz's hand, gathered her to him and lifted her off her feet.

'*Arrête*,' she said, half laughing. '*Lâche-moi*.' As he carefully put her down, Jake heard her whisper in Lucius's ear, 'Thank God you're safe!'

Jake's dream evaporated in an instant. He was embarrassed for even thinking it. Topaz and Lucius were clearly besotted with each other. With Jake, she behaved more like an older sister.

At last she untwined herself from the soldier and suddenly became serious. She swung round and checked that no one was watching. 'Quickly! We don't have much time and nowhere is safe. Follow me,' she said, setting off across the bridge towards Tiber Island. 'We can talk in the temple of Aesculapius. Then I have to get back before they notice I am gone. As you can see' – she indicated her armour – 'I had to go to some lengths to escape from the villa.' She knocked on her epaulettes to show that they were hollow. 'I don't know how you men carry great shoulders around

with you all day long. We females are far neater.'

The comment made Lucius smirk and flex his muscles. He caught up with her and took her hand, while Jake followed behind.

Topaz led them onto the island, through a dense copse of trees, across a small courtyard where the obelisk was situated (Jake noticed that it was inscribed with Egyptian hieroglyphics) to the temple. It was an impressive building: high, square and colonnaded on all sides. As she went up the steps, Topaz took one last look around, then the three of them slipped inside.

They found themselves in a large, dim chamber, lit only by the embers of two braziers and soft shafts of light filtering in through the high windows.

As Jake grew accustomed to the gloom, he noticed that there were people inside: most were lying on the floor, but some were moving amongst them with the quiet, careful tread of nurses.

'The sick come here for comfort and protection,' Topaz explained in a whisper. 'It is one of the most civilized places in the city.' As she passed one of the helpers, who looked angelic in flowing white robes, Topaz smiled warmly and received a serene nod in response. Jake scanned the row of patients, some

trembling, some hunched in pain. One in particular drew his attention: a youth – barely more than a boy, one-legged and painfully thin – who shook with fever.

Topaz led Jake and Lucius into the shadows in the far corner of the room. She stopped and leaned in close. '*Écoutez* – listen carefully, I am going to tell you what you must do.' She started to uncoil the chain from around her forearm. 'As I said, I have barely any time. Agata Zeldt, my "mother", has begun, little by little, to trust me, and it is imperative, *absolument imperatif*, for the safety of everyone – for the safety of the world, of history – that I retain that trust. Do you understand?'

Jake and Lucius nodded, the latter clenching his jaw with determination.

Topaz continued: 'She has been preparing for an event that she calls *the end of dominions*. You should know that she does not exaggerate. If her plan is to end dominions, that is what she will do – and on an unimaginable scale.'

'Topaz . . . your wrist!' Jake interrupted. He could now see that the chain was attached to a manacle that was so tight, it cut into her skin, leaving painful sores. He remembered a similar

device in her room on Vulcano and immediately put two and two together. 'They chain you up?' he asked in horror. 'You said she trusted you!'

'I said she has *begun* to trust me,' Topaz replied. 'Which, believe me, is more than I could ever have hoped for.' She spoke simply so as not to confuse Lucius. 'Jake, you know my mother and I were separated for many years? You know where I grew up, living with her greatest enemies? I have convinced her that I have changed, turned against all that. *Que je cherche la puissance noire.* That I am now seeking dark power.' She took a calming breath and gave the glimmer of a smile as she held up the end of the chain. 'Besides, as you can see, I found a way to undo the links. So, right now, I'm not chained up. I'm here with you.'

Jake said nothing. He nodded, but was secretly frightened by Topaz's manner: despite her warm welcome on the bridge, she seemed far steelier than when he first met her. Her face looked harder, more cunning. He couldn't help wondering if, in her attempts to convince her family, she really *had* changed, really *had* been tinged with some of her mother's malevolence.

'So listen,' she continued. 'I have only one key

piece of intelligence of my mother's plans: the first strike will take place tomorrow.' She looked at them both very seriously. 'It will all begin with what is called a *caedes publica* – a public murder.'

'A public murder?' repeated Jake, the notion sending a shiver of dread down the back of his neck.

'I don't know who or where – or indeed *how* this will lead to *the end of dominions*, but I have heard the phrase repeatedly.'

Jake nodded seriously.

'And you need to find out more.' Topaz took a deep breath. 'So, your instructions. My mother has a campaign room in the compound of her villa. Needless to say, it is heavily guarded and almost impossible to infiltrate. I have tried on two occasions; both times I nearly broke my neck – it is not a solo job. Tonight she is holding a masked ball. You must all attend. Cover yourselves well – especially you, Lucius. My mother will not recognize you – soldiers' faces mean nothing to her – but there could be guards from Vulcano. Try to gain access to this building and discover her plans.'

She unrolled three pieces of parchment and gave the first to Jake. He saw a list of names. 'Use those

aliases when you arrive. They are entirely credible and will match those on the guest register.' She passed him the next roll, which was covered in roughly drawn maps. 'This is the location of the villa, on the southwestern corner of the Palatine. And this' – she handed him the third – 'is a plan of the building. The party will take place in the arena in the centre of the compound. My mother's campaign room is on the far side in this domed structure . . .' She indicated it on the map. 'The only possible access is over the roofs. Understand?'

Jake and Lucius nodded.

'Tonight, there will be dinner followed by what my mother calls *ludi sanguinei* – blood games. I cannot say when is the best moment to make your move, but when the time is right, find the concealed door at the north end of the arena, next to a statue of Saturn. This key will unlock it . . .' She handed Jake a small bronze key. 'Inside there is a staircase that will take you to the top of the building, onto a private terrace. From here you can climb across the roofs to the campaign room. You will enter through the open skylight at the apex of the central dome here. It is high, so you will need to be lowered on ropes – that is why you must all go.'

'And what are we looking for?' Lucius asked. He was clearly a little out of his depth.

'Anything – find anything! For we are completely in the dark. We need to know about this public murder, and why Agata went to so much trouble to pick up the actor from Herculaneum – Austerio, I believe he is called – and if there is any connection between the two.'

Trying to sound as knowledgeable as possible, Jake chipped in, 'I saw a film once where spies used an actor to memorize secret information; maybe that's why they have him.'

'Who knows? I caught sight of him only briefly from my carriage window, when he was collected in Herculaneum. After we arrived in Rome he was taken to another part of the villa and I have not seen him since.' Topaz looked up at the high windows. Light was now streaming through them, illuminating a swirling constellation of particles. 'Morning is upon us and I must return.' Having given her lacerated wrist a chance to breathe, she started to wrap the chain around it once again. 'One last thing: tonight, *on no account* should any of you acknowledge me. You will not speak to me or even look at me. Is that understood?'

Jake nodded.

'If I cannot look at you tonight,' Lucius added with studied charm, 'I will ask a kiss of you now.'

At first Topaz shook her head, but when he pulled her to him and embraced her, she did not resist, melting into his arms. It went on for so long that Jake had to pretend to be interested in the mosaic floors.

Finally he coughed nervously. 'Just one last question,' he asked, still unable to look up. 'Who else will be at this party?'

At last Topaz was released. Her cheeks flushed, she took a moment to compose herself and straighten her clothes. 'What I call the *milliardaires affamés* – the hungry billionaires,' she replied. 'Dignitaries from all over the empire: merchants, lawyers, generals; people with one thing in common apart from their wealth – a desire to be *more* wealthy, by any possible means. It's incredible – Agata's lived here for just three years, but in a city famous for its snobbery, not a single person has questioned where she came from or who she is. She just appeared one day, with a load of gold. She headed for a vast villa on the Palatine, next to the emperor's. An old aristocrat had lived there for

decades, but she just kept increasing her offers of money until he finally moved out.'

'And *why* did no one question her?' Jake asked. He couldn't help but be intrigued by Agata Zeldt.

'Because she is the richest of them all; richer than the devil, they say.' Topaz looked stern, her mouth a tight line. 'Not just richer; crueller too.'

She turned and saw that the white-robed attendants had started handing out bread and water to their patients. 'Now, I must return.' She started to lead Jake and Lucius back towards the exit. Suddenly she stopped, unclasped a gold necklace from around her neck, and approached the poor one-legged youth Jake had seen before. With a kindly word, she dropped it into his trembling hand and closed his thin fingers around it.

She returned to Jake and Lucius, and they left the temple. Topaz hurriedly said her goodbyes.

'And remember,' she called back, 'you don't know me.' She replaced her helmet and hurried back over the Pons Fabricius into the city.

It was another half-hour before Charlie appeared for their agreed rendezvous. Jake quickly filled him in on their meeting with Topaz – explaining about the

public murder and showing him the papers she'd given him.

'I know this building from my research – it's one of the grandest in the city,' Charlie commented, studying the map. 'It even has its own miniature stadium. Let's go back to the bureau now and make plans. The place hasn't been used for a while and it was overrun with creepy-crawlies. Nathan is still cleaning up.'

He led them through the gates and along a series of streets until they came at last to a large open square bordered by striking buildings. 'The Roman Forum,' Charlie announced. 'The epicentre of the Empire. This is the seat of law and government.'

Jake and Lucius looked around. Some of the buildings were low and sprawling, others stood high over the square; but all were built from the same everlasting white marble that was Rome's trade-mark. They saw many finely dressed people: nearly everyone wore togas as white and pristine as the buildings around them.

'That's the Palatine hill,' said Charlie, pointing to a steep slope at one end; tier after tier of grand villas rose up its flanks. 'That's where Agata Zeldt lives. Fascinating fact: the word *palace* actually comes

from *Palatine*,' he added. 'At the other end is the Senate House – the *Curia Julia*, built by Julius Caesar in 44 BC, when he was at the height of his powers. All the senators meet there to pass their acts and laws. Quite incredible to think that it's the model of all parliaments to come.'

Jake looked up, surprised to see that the building was one of the plainest – just a simple box-like structure with a series of high windows. A meeting had just finished, and a mass of white-robed senators poured out through the doors, chatting as they filed down the steps.

Beside the Senate House stood a long, two-storey structure of distinctive red stone, fronted by a succession of *tabernae* – small shops mostly dealing in silver, gold and tin. 'This is the Basilica Aemilia,' Charlie informed them as he led them through a narrow doorway. Jake noticed a man with a hunched back and pinched face weighing small chunks of gold on a set of scales.

Inside, it was as cool and spacious as a cathedral. 'It's like a miniature forum . . .' Charlie gestured at the people dotted around the central nave. 'All sorts come here,' he said, indicating each group in turn. 'Moneylenders, lawyers, bankers, estate agents,

politicians – all plying their trade. It's a madhouse. In fact that's precisely why the bureau is located here.'

He led Jake and Lucius over to a dark recess between two pillars. He checked that no one was watching; then, with his foot, delicately depressed a brick in the base of one of the columns. Jake squinted down at the stone and could just make out a faint symbol that he recognized immediately: an hourglass with three atoms whizzing around it – the History Keepers' symbol. A second later, there was a click and a section of the wall opened. Charlie waved the others on into the dark chamber beyond, took one last look and followed, shutting the opening behind him. No one in the Basilica Aemilia was any the wiser.

Jake looked around. This entrance reminded him of his very first foray into the extraordinary world of the History Keepers – via a secret staircase below the Monument in the city of London. *These* stairs also spiralled down into the earth and were decorated with a series of murals depicting emperors, armies and processions (though rendered in mosaics rather than paint) that made Jake's spine tingle in anticipation.

'You said the bureau had not been in use for a while?' he asked Charlie, out of earshot of Lucius. 'No one works here?'

'You'll find that the further you go back in time,' Charlie whispered, 'the fewer local agents there are – these places are more *safe houses* than bureaux per se. It's to do with the limited number of people being able to travel to deep history.'

At the foot of the staircase there was another door concealed in the wall. Charlie knocked on it, using a special code.

'Charlie?' a voice asked from the other side.

'It is I.'

A key was turned in the lock and the door opened. 'Did you find her? Did she come?' Nathan asked immediately, seeing Jake and Lucius. He was wearing an apron and brandishing a feather duster.

'She's alive and well,' Charlie answered. 'We have an appointment tonight.'

'Good work, boys – brilliant work,' Nathan replied.

Jake stepped into a spacious vaulted chamber. It seemed welcoming and familiar, its dark wood panelling, and tables covered in maps, charts and globes completely at odds with the austere marble

of the city above them. The room was lined with shelves full of books from all ages, and there were two sets of bunk beds.

Nathan listened with keen interest as Jake repeated the story of his encounter with Topaz, asking questions and looking carefully at the maps she had given him.

When Jake was finished, Charlie pointed him towards the bunk in the far corner of the room. 'You can take that one there, next to that statue of Oceanus taming the waters.'

Jake happily obliged, slinging his bag down. He examined Oceanus, a hulking bearded figure carved in brilliant alabaster – as beautiful a piece of sculpture as Jake had ever seen, set casually in a corner of a History Keepers' bureau.

On the floor, sticking out below the bunk, was a large metal grille with a padlock. Beneath this, Jake could hear the rush of flowing water. 'Where does this lead to?' he asked, tapping the grille with his foot.

'It's an underground branch of the Aqua Virgo,' Charlie explained. 'One of the aqueducts supplying Rome with fresh water. It was built by Agrippa in AD 19, and comes eight miles from near Collartina,

east of the city, mostly underground, ending up at the baths of Agrippa half a mile down the road. Of course, we use it for our personal water supply.' He indicated a bucket on a chain next to the opening. 'Saves us having to go all the way upstairs when we fancy a drink.'

Jake peered down into the cavity and could just make out a wide, echoey tunnel.

Lucius was also inspecting the room apprehensively. There were many objects with which he was completely unfamiliar. 'What is this?' he asked, pointing to a globe that came from a more modern era.

'That is the world, but not as you know it,' said Charlie dismissively. It was best not to open the can of worms that was time travel, so he led Lucius over to a table of freshly prepared food. 'There's home-made muesli and a breakfast soufflé – prepared in an oven older than the ark – which has even me reaching for superlatives.'

After breakfast, as Lucius had a snooze, Charlie, Nathan and Jake sat down, first studying Topaz's map in greater detail, then poring over volumes of leather-bound annals that described all the key events of the previous decade. Amongst many things,

they learned in detail about the Emperor Tiberius and his eccentricities.

In his twenties he had shown himself to be a brave general, conquering swathes of land in Germania, as well as Dalmatia and Pannonia in south-eastern Europe. But he never enjoyed his position of supreme commander or grew accustomed to life in the largest city in the world. Soon he was regularly disappearing off to the island of Rhodes – much to the frustration of his senators. As he grew older, his paranoia had worsened, and a year ago he had left Rome for good in order to rule via Sejanus, his prefect, from a secret hideaway on the isle of Capri.

'What worries me,' Charlie murmured, 'is that, at the moment, Sejanus is not in the city either. He's on a state visit to the eastern frontier and is not due back for weeks. Certainly there are six hundred senators – but Rome is essentially leaderless. Which is interesting timing . . .'

In the afternoon, with their plans made, Nathan asked if anyone would mind if he went on a small shopping expedition. 'I feel the need to get under the skin of early Imperial fashion,' he announced. 'It's always been such a grey area.'

No one had any objections, so Nathan sloped off.

An hour later, he bustled in with armfuls of bulging linen sacks, his eyes shining with excitement. 'Revelatory!' he gasped. 'May I just say: *hemp* – it's just wrong, and usually I wouldn't touch it with a barge pole; but who knew how versatile it could be in the right hands?' He pulled out a couple of items from his bag to demonstrate. 'It's shabby, but *sooo* chic. At the other end of the scale' – he produced a silk tunic from another bag – 'if it's sheer gold you're after, may I introduce you to sea silk? It's startling. A revelation . . .' he added, a tear coming to his eye. 'Actually woven from the filaments of the *Pinna nobilis*, the rarest seashell in the Mediterranean.'

Nathan allowed Jake and Charlie to feel the fabric, then showed off some snakeskin boots and an assortment of chains and bangles that he described as 'very manly jewellery'.

Later, Charlie and Jake also popped out to visit a little shop that sold masks and other party paraphernalia. (Jake had noticed it down a narrow side street on their way from the Pons Fabricius that morning.) They came back with a whole collection, all similar in style to the ones worn by the actors in Herculaneum, with big cut-out mouths in either

happy or *sad* mode. Needless to say, Nathan and Lucius both wanted the same one – which looked like a ferocious warrior; but just as a heated row was about to erupt, Charlie pointed out that the colour didn't go with Nathan's skin tone and he dropped it like a hot potato.

They got changed into their smartest-looking outfits – togas with capes, as worn by the young noblemen of the city – and armed themselves with swords and daggers, concealed under their togas. Nathan and Jake each volunteered to carry a length of rope, which they hid by winding them around their waists. They all took a hateful swig of vinegar, Charlie left Mr Drake with a handful of nuts, and they lit torches and set off, ascending the spiral stair-case. At the top, Nathan checked through a spy-hole that the coast was clear, then pulled a catch to open the door and they filed through. Charlie closed the wall behind them.

The basilica was now half empty. A few clusters of people lingered in the fading afternoon sun. At one end, a handful listened uncertainly to a red-faced man on a podium speaking in rousing tones. He had obviously had too much to drink, for he suddenly staggered and fell down amongst his audience.

Nathan led the others out into the Roman Forum. Dusk was descending and a warm pink light picked out the villas of the Palatine. It was towards these grand and ancient buildings that the intrepid young agents set off, each clutching his mask and silently pondering what lay in store for them that evening.

15 DIABOLICAL DINNER

The villa that Agata Zeldt called home clung to the southwestern side of the Palatine, over-looking the Circus Maximus on one side and the great field of Mars on the other. Jake and his companions approached it, first up a steep slope from the southern end of the Forum, then along a wide, tranquil boulevard that snaked between the grand residences of this most ancient and revered district. The air was much fresher up here, and sweetened by the fragrance of the pines. It was quieter too, away from the bustle of the city below; they heard only the sounds of running water mixed with the muffled conversations of well-to-do people behind the walls of their luxury compounds.

Occasionally, the tranquillity was broken by a carriage rolling up the hill or by the grunts of slaves

bearing litters – all evidently transporting illustrious guests to Agata's party – before disappearing down a driveway near the crest.

As they approached the gated entrance, which was lit by a succession of tapers and guarded by all sorts of soldiers and attendants, Nathan stopped in the shadows behind a tree.

'We should go in two groups,' he whispered. 'Draw less attention to ourselves. Lucius and I will enter first. You two follow in fifteen minutes. Good luck.'

Nathan took a deep breath, put on his mask, puffed up his chest, clicked the bones in his hands and set off. Lucius went through the same routine, in a more exaggerated fashion, then followed. Jake and Charlie watched them stride up the narrow drive, give their fake names to an attendant and disappear through the gates.

To kill some time, Jake and Charlie wandered up to the summit and looked down at the Circus Maximus. The sight of it filled Jake with wonder. From above, it looked even more sensational than it had appeared on their way into the city the day before. Illuminated by torches set around its track of white sand, it had an otherworldly quality, as if it

were the stadium of the gods themselves.

Some kind of training exercise was taking place there: a couple of chariots, each harnessed to a team of galloping horses, were flying around the track as a coach shouted instructions from the side-lines.

'There's a big race tomorrow,' Charlie explained. 'One of the biggest of the year. By tomorrow morning, the whole of Rome will be here.'

Jake could also hear distant shrieks and roars of animals. He couldn't tell where they were coming from.

'Wild beasts,' said Charlie. He pointed to the great stone island in the centre of the arena that divided the track in two. 'They're caged under the *spina* there. They'll be bears, tigers, perhaps even a rhinoceros – animals from every corner of the world.' He screwed up his face with distaste. 'They parade them before the chariot races or use them for their gory entertainments.'

As Jake looked more carefully, he noticed workmen erecting a wooden balustrade around the edge of the island. 'Do people stand up there too?' he asked.

'Oh yes, the *crème de la crème* watch from the *spina*. Rome's six hundred-odd senators. It's

symbolic, you see: *standing on top of the beasts*. To show the people that they are kings – not just of the world – but of all nature. Although actually it's a new tradition; they used to sit beside the *pulvinar* over there.' Charlie pointed towards a stone structure opposite – a temple with columns fronted by a wide terrace. 'That's the imperial box, where the emperor sits.'

Again they heard distant roars from the *spina*, carried up on the warm night air. Charlie's eyes lingered for a moment. 'Anyway, we should go now,' he said at last.

They slipped on their masks – Jake's had a cheerful smile, while Charlie's looked a little confused – and headed up the drive. A doorman stepped forward to take their names. Jake gave his in a steady voice that belied his terror. A thick-set guard opened the gates and they were both ushered inside.

A line of slaves, each standing rigidly to attention, heads bowed, marked the way through a series of wide corridors towards the sounds of the party. At last they emerged into the open air.

They were greeted with such a spine-chilling sight that Jake faltered. A hundred frozen masks turned in unison to scrutinize the new arrivals. Jake

felt beads of sweat running down his forehead under his own mask.

'All right?' Charlie whispered, laying a reassuring hand on his shoulder. Jake nodded and took a deep breath. Gradually the masked faces turned back to their own groups and the chatter resumed.

It was an extraordinary space, long and colonnaded, echoing the form of the Circus Maximus below, but in miniature. It was open to the stars and adorned with eye-catching statues. Dinner tables were set up along the sides, with elegant, silk-covered couches. (Jake had learned that Romans – the rich ones at any rate – did not use dining chairs but ate lying down!) In the centre, steps led down to an arena, elliptical in shape, bordered by a low wall and illuminated by lanterns. Here, no doubt, Jake realized with a shiver, Agata's *ludi sanguinei*, or blood games, would later take place.

At the very edges, half in the shadows of the stone columns, musicians played lutes, flutes and lyres, and a small army of slaves waited discreetly to attend to the whims of the guests.

'Monster she may be, but it's undeniable that Agata Zeldt has taste!' a voice said from behind a mask. It was Nathan, excited to find himself at such

a lavish event. Behind him, Lucius's hulking frame looked ill at ease. 'She has a sense of theatre, of *grand guignol*, which is quite refreshing after her brother's gloomy Gothicism.' Nathan held up his silver goblet. 'May I recommend the honey and watermelon cocktails? They're chilled perfection, as you might say, Charlie. No doubt as icy as our hostess.'

'And where *is* our hostess?' Charlie asked anxiously. 'Any sign?'

'Not to mention Topaz,' Jake added. He had already scanned all the females in the garden.

'Well, *there* is the statue of Saturn.' Charlie nodded towards a sculpture under the colonnade: a chunky, bearded deity holding a torch in his hand. 'There's a door next to it.'

Just then they heard a loud roll of drums followed by a fanfare of horns, and three figures appeared through the grand archway at the far end of the arena; there were gasps of wonder from the guests, followed by a spontaneous ripple of applause.

Leading the group was their hostess herself, dressed in a fantastically devilish costume inspired by dark birds of paradise. A bodice of feathers clung

to her lithe frame and a bustle sprouted magnificently from her behind. A collar of long peacock quills encased her head and set off her flame-coloured hair. She wore a half-mask – in deep ultramarine – exposing her cruel, bloodless lips.

'Well, of course she's playing fast and loose with every fashion under the sun,' whispered Nathan in awe, 'but what a sensational result!'

'Wake-up call!' said Charlie, clicking his fingers in front of Nathan to get his attention. 'She murders for pleasure and she's about to destroy the world as we know it!'

Jake was not looking at Agata; he was staring at the two figures behind her. His lip curled in disgust at the sight of the blond youth on Agata's left, whom he recognized immediately – even behind his spotted mask – as the arrogant Leopardo. But his heart went out to the chained and manacled figure the boy was pulling along as if she were a circus animal: Topaz.

Lucius started snorting and flexing his muscles, and Nathan had to hold him back. 'Remember what you and Jake were told? We don't know her.'

Once again, Jake couldn't help thinking how different she looked from the bright, vivacious

Topaz he had first met in London. Earlier that morning she had been steelier; now she was almost pathetic.

Agata held up her hands majestically and said a few words in Latin, her voice soft and deadly as poison. '*Welcome, all. So happy you could join us in our humble home,*' Charlie translated with a roll of the eyes. Then she clapped her hands together and instructed everyone to recline and enjoy the feast.

'That's our cue,' Nathan said, nodding at the others.

While the guests took their positions on the couches, the slaves brought in chargers of food. In the confusion, the four boys surreptitiously made their way towards the concealed doorway next to the statue of Saturn.

They had nearly reached it when a shadow loomed up ahead of them. Jake's heart stopped when he realized that the figure was wearing a leopard mask and was trailing the unfortunate Topaz behind him.

'*Sedete,*' he said in a silky voice, motioning for them to sit.

There was some space amongst a group of diners reclining around the nearest table. The boys

couldn't very well refuse. Charlie thanked Leopardo with a gracious bow and they took their places as calmly as they were able. Jake noticed that Topaz looked terrified, but her half-brother gave no indication that he suspected anything, and lay down with his back to them.

As she took a seat next to the monster, Topaz quickly glanced around. Her eyes made contact with Jake's. She glared at him for a moment – in fear or friendship, he couldn't tell – then turned away.

Jake looked at the other diners; they were an unappealing lot, arrogant and overfed, gossiping and laughing, one eye fixed on the new arrivals. They had half pushed up their masks in anticipation of food and motioned for the boys to do the same. Keeping their faces hidden as much as possible, they followed suit.

Suspended just above the table – and, indeed, Jake noticed, above *every* table – was a little cage containing a small bird with vivid yellow plumage singing an exquisite song. Charlie was immediately taken with it and tried to reach his fingers in, but the creature was unfriendly, puffing its feathers and shrinking away from him. Suddenly something far more alarming caught Charlie's attention. 'Hell's

bells,' he muttered under his breath as a slave approached with a great platter and set it down on the table in front of them, explaining what it was.

'Baked flamingo and swan surprise,' Charlie translated in a horrified whisper.

The guests were all cooing with delight, but Jake could barely believe his eyes: from the roasted bodies of two giant birds (still covered in charred feathers) two necks – one pink and one white – rose up to create the shape of a heart between them, their beaks touching in a delicate kiss of death.

'I wonder what the surprise is?' Nathan asked out of the side of his mouth. Usually he was quite imperturbable, but even he looked a little worried.

The attendant plunged a knife into the side of each bird. From within came a chorus of high-pitched cries, and out flew a handful of live nightingales. Lucius stood up and half drew his sword in fright, much to the amusement of their fellow diners, but Nathan pulled him down again. From every table, amidst applause and cheers, nightingales took off, fluttering in confusion into the sky.

'Barbaric,' Charlie whispered under his breath, shaking his head. 'Absolutely barbaric.'

The culinary horrors did not end there. Dish after dish of macabre recipes were brought out. Mostly they had an avian theme: turtledove ragout with pomegranates, peacock stewed in honey and damsons, and ostrich flambé; but there were other recipes to bring shudders of distaste: jellyfish and eggs, pickled sea urchins, and eels stuffed with sprats.

Lucius ate nearly everything, which meant that Nathan felt obliged to do the same. Jake bravely tried to swallow something, so as not to attract too much attention, but Charlie ate practically nothing, and became more and more upset by what he called 'the dreadful savagery of the rich'.

Towards the end of the meal, a figure appeared at the main door: a tall, strange-looking man with a gaunt, unmasked face and a long plaited beard. Jake recognized him, but couldn't remember where from. Eventually he started to weave his way between the tables until he was at Agata's side. She received him with a nod and he leaned down to whisper in her ear.

Jake suddenly realized: 'It's the man from the laboratory in Vulcano,' he said quietly. They had seen him working in the room with the

foul-smelling plants. Nathan and Charlie looked over.

'No doubt he has come to assist her with *the end of dominions,*' the latter commented, his gloom sharpened by hunger.

After the dishes had been cleared away, an unusual-looking man wearing a wig of curling red hair – a master of ceremonies of some kind – stepped into the middle of the arena and made an announcement in a deep, gravelly voice. What he had said soon became clear – for at each table the guests opened their birdcages to let loose the yellow songbirds. They flew up in unison, circled one way, then the other, before finally settling on the man, so that he looked like a giant bird himself. To complete this image, he started to rise up into the air as if he were indeed flying. Jake realized that he was actually being raised up by some underground mechanism, but it was such an eye-catching trick that the amazed audience immediately stood up to get a better look. It was at this moment that Topaz turned and nodded at the others to indicate that now was the time to go.

No one noticed the four boys disappear into the shadows of the colonnade and creep over to

the statue of Saturn. In a flash Nathan had produced Topaz's key, unlocked the door, and led the others inside.

Nathan and Jake breathed a sigh of relief as they unwound the lengths of ropes and slung them over their shoulders. They made their way up the narrow steps, flight after flight, their footsteps echoing around the dark stairwell, until finally they came to a door. At first it would not open, and Charlie feared it might also be locked; but Nathan gave it an almighty shove, burst through, and the others followed him out onto the terrace.

They were at one of the highest points in the city and the view – 360 degrees of it – was astounding. Under a perfect evening sky of midnight blue, the white marble of the city extended into the distant purple haze. It seemed much more peaceful at night, especially viewed from this vantage point, and a warm breeze swirled around them with a faint whistle.

'Well I'll be blowed,' said Charlie excitedly, spotting a distinctive shape on one side of the terrace. 'An original Montgolfier, if I'm not mistaken.'

Jake, Nathan and Lucius turned to see a large

basket connected to a mammoth bundle of material in gold and indigo.

'Montgolfier? Montgolfier?' Nathan pondered. 'I know the name . . . Remind me.'

Charlie sighed and shook his head. 'Nathan, sometimes I wonder if you've done any basic research at all. The Montgolfier brothers, inventors of the world's first hot-air balloon?' As Jake and Nathan went to investigate, Charlie carried on, 'Actually, that's not strictly speaking true. The Chinese had a go in the era of the Three Kingdoms, around 200 AD. And I've heard rumours that the Nazca of Peru might have got there even earlier. But October 1783 – four years after the French Revolution – was the official date of the first manned flight. Whatever way you look at it, it's still *totally* out of place here. Agata Zeldt truly has no respect for history. Can you imagine this taking off across the skies of ancient Rome?'

Jake found the idea entrancing: a hot-air balloon from the other end of history wafting over the city, to the amazement of all.

With Nathan leading the way, the four of them hauled themselves over the balustrade at the back of the terrace and surveyed the dark geometric rooftop landscape.

'There,' said Jake, identifying, in the furthest corner, the domed building that Topaz had told them housed Agata's campaign room. They set off across the roof tiles, four silhouettes against the ultramarine sky. Occasionally they reached an impasse, a wide gap between the buildings, and would have to double back and find a different route. At one point they passed a skylight. From it emerged a strange fluttering sound that intrigued Jake. He couldn't resist kneeling down and peering through the bars.

A dim light from below illuminated his face as he examined the large, empty chamber. There was a shape on the floor – some kind of creature, tied to a metal post, lying perfectly still on a bed of dark crimson. Then the sickening truth dawned on him: the creature was the half-eaten remains of a man, its bed a pool of dry blood. Suddenly there was an ear-splitting squawk, a rush of air, and a bird almost the size of Jake threw itself at the bars, thrusting its head between them and snapping at him with its razor-sharp beak.

Jake cried out, stumbling back across the tiles and falling heavily. The others stopped and turned as he picked himself up. Now the heads of three

savage vultures were straining through the bars, shrieking like banshees.

'Such charming pets our hostess has,' Nathan commented drily. 'They make her brother's snakes look positively cuddly.'

Jake stared at the birds with disgust as he edged his way along the tiles and caught up with the others.

Agata's campaign headquarters were housed in a solid, square, domed structure. Its far walls dropped straight down to join the sheer cliff face of the Palatine; on the near side, it was separated from its neighbours by a gap of nearly two metres. The boys gingerly made their way over to the drop and looked down. Below them stood two hulking men guarding the double entrance doors. Round the side, they saw two high windows, both tiny and barred. Topaz had explained that the only way in was through the skylight at the top of the dome; they could see a soft light shining up through it. But to reach it, they first had to get across the gap.

'I'll go first,' Nathan whispered to the others. He took a few steps back, then ran, vaulting over the divide and landing perfectly, with barely a sound, on the other side. He peered down: the guards were

talking to each other, oblivious to what was going on above their heads. Lucius went next, landing in an elaborate somersault and making it look like child's play. Charlie followed, showing no fear at all. Then it was Jake's turn. He didn't like it one bit, but kept his fears to himself. He stepped back, took a deep breath and lunged forward into the air. As the void opened up beneath him, he had a sudden premonition of disaster. His foot came down short, landing on the edge. His eyes widened as he teetered on the brink, then Charlie grabbed him and pulled him forward. The sentries failed to notice the light dusting of stone that fell down into the gap.

They tiptoed across the roof, clambered up the side of the dome and peered inside. Below them was an octagonal room with a black and white floor of shiny marble that reflected the light from a series of low-hanging lanterns. In the centre stood a circular table with a map spread across its tapestry cover. Even from this distance Jake could make out the shapes of continents: Europe, Africa and Asia. It was mostly emerald green, but there were blocks of other colours. Other tables were dotted around the room, many piled up with plans, tables and diagrams.

'Can I go first?' Jake asked the others. He was embarrassed about what had just happened on the roof and wanted to prove himself. 'I'm very good with ropes,' he lied.

For once, Nathan couldn't find a reason to disagree. 'Sure.' He shrugged. 'What's the worst that could happen?'

'Well, the worst that could happen,' said Charlie, pushing his glasses up his nose, 'is that he falls, crashing onto that map, and alerts the whole villa to our whereabouts.'

'It was rhetorical, Charlie.' Nathan gritted his teeth. 'You don't have to answer that question every time I ask it.'

Jake was harnessed to the rope, and Lucius, by far the strongest of them, lowered him down. As he descended, Jake noticed that the inside of the dome was painted dark blue and covered with symbols of the constellations over faint golden grids of latitude and longitude.

His foot edged towards the chart, his toes touching down on Italy – on Rome itself; indeed, on a tiny replica of the Circus Maximus. Only now did Jake realize that the map was not flat, but a three-dimensional relief. He carefully leaped down onto

the floor, before turning round to have a closer look. It was a beautifully realized miniature of the western world in AD 27. It illustrated, in breathtaking detail, not only the terrain – the mountains, deserts and forests – but many of the famous landmarks, from the pyramids of Egypt to the ancient stone circles of Britain.

But the map was not only geographical; it was scattered with legions of armies. Battalions of minute soldiers (it was these that had formed the blocks of colour Jake had seen from above) were stationed everywhere – from the white peaks of the Alps to the plains of Persia; from the deserts of the Sahara to the wintry forests of Scandinavia. And each soldier, of the thousands that populated the map, wore the same uniform: the familiar armour of the Hydra.

Charlie was the next to descend, followed shortly by Nathan (Lucius was showing off again, proving he could lower two people simultaneously). Once he was on the ground, Nathan called up to him, 'Maintain that position! We may need to leave at any second.'

'Anything you say, sir,' Lucius replied with a smirk, and sat down with his legs dangling through the skylight.

'I've said it already and I'll say it again,' Nathan said, glancing up at the constellations on the inside of the dome, 'you have to admire Agata's chutzpah. The world is not enough for her – she wants the *universe*.'

'Good gracious, you're right,' Charlie replied, examining it in greater detail. 'She's renamed Scorpio after herself, and Leopardo has been substituted for Ursa Major.'

Jake hadn't noticed before, but now he could clearly see their names inscribed in curling gold letters across the blue sky. He also realized that another section was in the process of being repainted – no doubt to include the new member of the family: Topaz.

Nathan and Charlie turned their attention to Agata's map – in particular to the armies. 'Unless Agata Zeldt plans to produce half a million soldiers out of thin air,' Nathan commented, 'I guess her plan is to somehow take command of the Roman army.'

'I'd say that was about the size of it,' Charlie concurred.

'And how big is the Roman army?' Jake asked. 'I mean, how many men in each of those divisions?'

Charlie shrugged and whistled through his teeth. 'Well, in the last hundred years the army has grown tenfold, from a haphazard collection of forces scattered here and there into a hardened and super-efficient machine, capable of conquering anyone.'

'He's right,' Nathan agreed, picking up one of the miniature soldiers and inspecting it. 'Look at poor old Mithridates and the Persians. One of the most ancient and revered nations in history, wiped out in a decade.'

'Regarding actual number' – Charlie was adding it up in his head – 'there must be at least twenty-five legions with roughly five thousand infantrymen in each, and probably three hundred *auxilia* regiments – including the navy, cavalry, et cetera, as well as the multitude of foreign conscripts. Which all adds up to about 400,000 fighting men.'

'In short,' Nathan concluded, 'enough to enslave the western world and have a good stab at taking over the rest.' Then he added with a theatrical arch of his eyebrows, '*The end of dominions.*'

'But how is she planning to get control of the Roman army?' Jake asked.

'That is the question we must answer,' Charlie replied. 'Buttering up a few corrupt lawyers and

generals with flamingo surprise and eels stuffed with sprats is only going to get you so far.'

'And the other question is' – Nathan held up the tiny soldier – '*who* was responsible for these gaudy uniforms? It's a travesty on every level. If you're going to take over the world, get the *look* right first. Wouldn't you agree?'

Charlie snatched the figure, replaced it on the map and suggested they should all stop talking and start looking. He and Jake began to go through the piles of papers to see if they could find any more information on *the end of dominions* or this *public murder* that Topaz had told them about, while Nathan opened all the doors that led off from the chamber to see if there was any sign of the actor Austerio.

Their various searches bore no immediate results: Nathan could find only storerooms, while the charts and papers turned out to be either irrelevant or indecipherable. Only one thing caught Jake's attention: a drawing of seven golden eggs, with the word *Counters* scrawled underneath. He remembered, from Agata's suite in Vulcano, something with an identical illustration.

'Does this mean anything to you?' he said, holding it up to Nathan.

Nathan glanced over, but made no sense of it. He shrugged, suggesting that it was of no importance; before turning his attention to a wall mirror, its reflective properties derived from a layer of mercury behind glass. As he admired his teeth, he claimed it was the most ingenious and charming thing he had seen all year.

After about twenty minutes, Lucius gave an urgent whistle from above. 'Someone's coming.'

A moment later, they heard the sound of a key in the lock and muffled voices. They looked at each other in alarm.

'Raise the ropes now!' Nathan commanded Lucius. 'Everyone else, under here . . .' He went over to the map table, lifted the tapestry cover and pushed Jake and Charlie underneath. The ropes shot up through the skylight and disappeared. Nathan squeezed into the dark space under the table with the other two. In unison, without prompting, all three silently drew their daggers as they heard the door opening and footsteps approaching.

Jake and Nathan could see what was going on through a hole in the tapestry. They breathed sighs of relief when they saw not guards but a couple of slaves, each carrying a tray of food – some familiar

items from dinner. The two men headed across the room, one reaching down to pull on a lever. Immediately a section of black and white floor rose up, revealing a set of steps that led down into a room underneath.

The two slaves descended. Moments later the boys heard a voice. It was so deep and fruity – so like the voice of an actor – that they were in no doubt as to its owner. Presently the slaves returned empty handed and, leaving the trapdoor open, walked back across the room, locking the door behind them.

Jake, Nathan and Charlie crawled out of their hiding place as Lucius appeared grinning in the aperture above. 'They've gone,' he said in his version of a whisper.

Nathan put his finger to his mouth to signal for everyone to be silent. He led the others down the small flight of steps and stopped in front of a red velvet curtain. Behind it, the distinctive, almost comical voice had started up again, practising the same phrase over and over using slightly different tones each time: '*Veni, vidi, vici.*'

It was one of the few pieces of Latin that Jake

knew – 'I came, I saw, I conquered' – spoken, he was certain, by Julius Caesar after invading some new country.

With the tip of his dagger, Nathan drew back the curtain to reveal the man in the room beyond. He looked both magnificent and ridiculous. On the one hand he was tall, aristocratic-looking, dressed in a dark purple toga, with a laurel wreath on his head. On the other, he kept pulling peculiar faces at himself in a mirror, doing odd exercises with his mouth, while striking poses and waving around a half-eaten leg of baked flamingo.

Jake and Nathan were trying hard not to laugh, but Charlie's expression was serious. The moment he set eyes on Austerio, he understood what was going on: the facial likeness, the purple toga, the oratory. 'Tiberius,' he murmured. 'He's going to impersonate the Emperor Tiberius.'

'What?' whispered Nathan, his smile suddenly evaporating.

'The emperor is a recluse, remember?' Charlie explained. 'He lives on Capri. He has barely been seen in public for years, but this man is the spitting image of him.'

As Jake craned to get a better look, he knocked

Nathan's dagger from his hand and it dropped with a clang on the floor.

Austerio – for it was surely he – swung round, gasping in horror as the three boys swept in. Perhaps if they had been unarmed he might have reacted differently; but as they came towards him, he waved his arms, moaning and rolling his eyes like some character from a Greek tragedy. Realizing that gestures alone were not going to save him, he flung his flamingo drumstick at them, then his plate of food, along with a couple of candlesticks. Nathan finally managed to clap a hand over his ranting mouth.

'*Ssh!* Listen, we're not here to hurt you,' he told him. 'We're friends. *Amici sumus.* You are Austerio – *tu es Austerio, amicus Ficium* – Fico the Fantastic.'

Austerio had been struggling and trying to yell through Nathan's fingers, but on hearing his name, and then that of his friend (or enemy), he gradually calmed down. Eventually Nathan removed his hand.

Austerio collected himself, rearranging his few strands of hair before replying tersely, 'Fico is not fantastic, it is *I* who is fantastic.' And to demonstrate the point, he struck a dramatic pose, showing

his face first front-on and then in profile.

'You speak English?' Charlie asked, bemused.

'Of course.' The actor shrugged. 'I have a thousand talents. Fico has none.'

Nathan picked up a bound book from the table. '*Latin–English dictionary*,' he read from the spine, then opened it and looked inside. 'Published 1590 – somewhat advanced for Roman times?' he commented to the others before turning back to Austerio. 'Did Agata Zeldt tell you to learn English? How long have you known her?'

Austerio carefully examined them all before finally answering with a petulant shrug, 'Who are you and what business have you here?'

Nathan and Charlie looked at each other blankly, but Jake jumped straight in: 'We're writing an epic poem. About you – about all your achievements.'

'An epic poem?' Austerio asked, immediately interested.

'We're your greatest fans,' Jake assured him with a bow. 'Your most loyal supporters. In Herculaneum, we have watched every one of your performances – haven't we?'

Charlie and Nathan nodded eagerly.

The actor was hooked. 'But you're just children,'

he said patronizingly, but couldn't resist adding, 'Really? Every performance?'

'All the classics,' Charlie chipped in. 'Plautus, Terence . . .'

'You saw my Phormio?' he asked, striking another heroic pose. 'My towering Greek commander?'

'It was so moving,' Nathan stated with absolute sincerity, 'I nearly threw myself on my sword.'

'By Jupiter! If that's how you find my comedies, my tragedies must be *unbearable.*'

'You have no idea.' Nathan shook his head and put his hand on his heart – once again choosing the wrong side.

Suddenly Austerio frowned and glanced towards the stairs, then leaned forward to whisper, '*Periculosus est hic* – but it is dangerous here. If you are found, they will think you are spies. How came you in?'

'We followed you all the way to Rome,' said Jake, 'then waited outside the villa for an opportunity to see you.'

Moved by such devotion, Austerio sighed, his eyes welling with tears.

Then, not to be outdone in the acting stakes,

Charlie added, 'For our own sanity, you must tell us what it is you are doing here. Herculaneum is barren without you.'

At first Austerio was reluctant to discuss the matter, but after a good deal of coaxing, his vanity got the better of him and he began to talk – first in snippets, then in ever-increasing torrents. He spoke of how he had first met his *patroness* – as he called Agata – six months ago; of how she had admired his talent and wined and dined him in all the fashionable eateries of the bay of Naples; of her desire for him to learn her peculiar language to make him an even bigger star. He recounted how she had picked him up in Herculaneum and transported him – by ship and then by carriage, in the lap of luxury – to Rome.

'That's all very exciting,' Nathan butted in, 'but what exactly are you doing here?'

Austerio looked down his nose at them. 'I am here to give the performance of my life; to play none other than the Emperor Tiberius – it is a matter of national security.'

Charlie nudged Jake. 'Didn't I say so?'

'That's right. I, the humble Austerio,' he declared, 'just a small-town boy from the wrong side

of the Apennines, using my oceanic talent to save my beloved country!'

'*National security?*' Charlie repeated. '*Save your beloved country?* What do you mean?'

Austerio leaned in close and whispered, 'Dear boys, I hate to be the bearer of bad tidings, but an uprising is afoot. A bloody revolution across the Empire, ten times more deadly than that of Spartacus. The world is on the brink of calamity!' He put his hand on his heart – choosing the correct side, unlike Nathan, Jake noticed. 'But I shall be playing my part to bring safety back to the people.'

Needless to say, when questioned about exactly how he would be doing this, he couldn't give a straight answer – mumbling something about *an empire needing its emperor* – and when asked who would be leading this revolt, he also looked blank.

They were about to ask him all sorts of other questions when they heard a bell tolling.

'That's it,' Austerio gasped. 'The fourth hour. They'll be coming for me at any moment. You must go,' he said, pushing them out of the room. 'They will think you are spies, and have no mercy.'

'Coming for you?' asked Nathan.

'I am to make *a regal appearance* at the party,'

Austerio said, 'before the big day tomorrow.'

'*Tomorrow?*' Jake, Nathan and Charlie repeated in unison. 'What's tomorrow?'

'My first *public* show. I am to appear at the games at the Circus Maximus. Now go . . .' He ushered them up the stairs. 'Leopardo will be here any second and I must get ready.'

Hearing this name, the young agents looked at each other. None of them fancied bumping into Leopardo. They quickly said their goodbyes, promised to look out for Austerio the next day, and charged back up the stairs.

'And be careful, boys.' He sighed, putting his hand on his heart again. 'I will do everything in my power to prevent the revolution, but Rome is not a safe place to be.'

Charlie whistled up to Lucius, who lowered the two ropes. Nathan quickly climbed up first, without any help. Charlie took the second rope. Jake was always surprised that Charlie, who spoke twenty languages and understood quantum physics, was so agile as well. He had none of Nathan's style but he had shinned up the rope in no time at all.

In contrast, Jake, even with Lucius's help, struggled to pull himself up. He had nearly made it

to the skylight when he heard the sound of a key in the lock below. In a flash, the door flew open and Leopardo strode into the room.

Jake had stopped breathing. He was hanging in midair from a spinning, creaking rope.

16 ANDROMEDA AND THE SEA MONSTER

Nathan, Charlie and Lucius, their faces hovering in the darkness above the skylight, watched in horror as Leopardo strode over to the trapdoor and called out to Austerio. They hoped he would go down the steps so that they could pull Jake to safety. But he simply waited, pouting at himself – just like Nathan – in the mercury wall mirror, until Austerio appeared.

The actor immediately caught sight of Jake, suspended in the dome, and gasped out loud. Jake lost his grip and slipped down towards the table, the coarse rope burning his palms as he did so.

The boys were sure that it would end in disaster, but Austerio acted quickly, pretending that he was simply shocked by the sight of his reflection in the

mirror. He muttered something about everything being off centre and asked Leopardo to straighten his crown of laurels. As the latter complied with a curl of his lip, Jake was hauled up towards the skylight.

He was almost there when Leopardo clapped his hands and announced that they must leave immediately. At this moment, disaster struck: Jake's mask, which he had tucked inside his toga, fell out. He tried in vain to grab it with one hand, then with a foot. As it spiralled down towards the floor, Austerio started speaking again, this time complaining loudly about the cut of his tunic.

Losing patience, Leopardo barked that there was nothing wrong with it and headed towards the door. Suddenly he stopped dead, catching sight of the mask on the floor. He picked it up and examined it, looking at Austerio – and then up at the dome. There was nothing there: just a dark patch of sky framed by the skylight. He opened the door and ushered the actor through.

From the rooftop, four silhouettes, all breathing great sighs of relief, watched Leopardo and Austerio cross the courtyard below and enter the villa.

For a short while they stood there in the darkness, mulling everything over.

Charlie was the first to speak. 'He said that the Circus Maximus was to be his first *public* show.'

'Yep.' Nathan nodded seriously. 'I heard that too.' He turned to Jake. 'And what did Topaz say? Everything will begin with a *public* murder?'

Suddenly it dawned on Jake – a shocking and terrible idea. '*He's* going to be murdered? Austerio?'

'Not Austerio,' Nathan corrected him. 'Tiberius.' He raised his eyebrows. 'I know my Roman history is not as good as yours, Charlie, but ever since Spartacus, isn't everyone in the empire paranoid about another rebellion?'

'Spartacus,' Lucius suddenly chipped in. 'I've heard of him.'

Nathan turned to Jake. 'He was this rogue gladiator who got all the slaves to rise up against their masters. What better way to spark *the end of dominions* than by assassinating the emperor and then blaming it on a bunch of "rebels" who probably don't even exist. It would be mayhem. A civil war could erupt within days.'

Charlie was shaking his head. 'It's a good theory but it doesn't make sense. Why would Agata bother to teach Austerio English if she was going to do away with him?'

'Well, we don't have much else to go on' –
Nathan shrugged – 'except that *something* is going to
happen at the Circus Maximus tomorrow. So I
suggest we get back to the bureau and work out
what we're going to do about it.'

He led his companions back across the roofs.
They jumped down onto Agata's private terrace and
descended the dark staircase to the door that went
into the arena. The party had become a good deal
more raucous and the music much louder.

'Here – you wear this,' Nathan said to Jake, passing him his mask. He turned to the others and
whispered, 'Let's get out of here as quickly as we
can.'

Charlie agreed, but Jake said nothing. He hated
the thought of leaving Topaz again. Just as Nathan
was about to open the door, silence suddenly fell on
the other side. Then they heard Agata saying something in Latin, ending with the phrase: '*Salutate
imperatorem!*'

It was followed by a chorus of respectful cheers
and shouts of '*Salve, Caesar!*'

Jake, Charlie and Lucius put on their masks,
while Nathan pulled up the hood of his cape. He
edged open the door, and the four of them slipped

through. The guests were all on their feet (at least, the men were; some of the women were still reclining) as Austerio, 'the Emperor Tiberius', passed regally among them, bestowing nods here and there and occasionally offering his fat, bejewelled hand to be kissed. Jake had half imagined that he might play the part like a pantomime character, so he was surprised by how subtle and convincing he was in the role. The 'emperor' was shown to a throne next to Agata's, and everyone else sat down again. This was when Jake realized that Topaz's place was empty. He searched all around for her, but she was nowhere to be seen.

'Let's go,' Nathan said in his ear, guessing the reason for his delay. 'Topaz knows where we are – she will contact us if she needs to.'

They crept along in the shadow of the colonnade towards the exit. They had almost reached it when the musicians struck up again. The horn players and the drummers started marching, in time to the music, towards the edge of the arena. There was a ripple of excitement, and everyone started whispering in anticipation of what was to come.

The music grew even louder. Then suddenly the stone floor at the centre of the arena began to open;

first there was a strip of darkness, then a gaping cavity. Out of this rose a vast misshapen boulder that looked like it had been torn from a wild seashore. On top of this, in a pose straight from Roman mythology, lay a nymph, manacled to the rock, her face hidden by a mass of soaking hair. She was perfectly still, as if under a spell; and Jake realized, with a lurch of horror, that it was Topaz.

He guessed that they were about to witness Agata Zeldt's *ludi sanguinei* – the blood games that Topaz had mentioned earlier. 'What are they going to do to her?' he asked, the words sticking in his throat.

'Come on . . .' Nathan gently tugged him on. 'Remember what she told you? We must not look at her.'

But Jake was not listening and shook Nathan's hand off. Lucius was rooted to the spot, his eyes fixed on the spectacle. Charlie was also reluctant to leave, and in truth, Nathan felt the same: he knew that his duty lay with the History Keepers, but he was as concerned as the others for his adopted sister.

The floor continued to rise; the boulder was now surrounded by a rocky pool, foaming and churning as if alive with fish. The whole section rose up until it was level with the audience, then stopped.

The guests were now waiting, agog, shifting this way and that to get the best view. Jake saw Agata Zeldt removing her mask to reveal a face twisted into a sadistic smile, while Leopardo, standing behind her, dug his fingers into her shoulders.

The music was deafening now – the horns blared and the drums beat like thunder. Jake felt the hairs stand up on the back of his neck. Suddenly there was a gasp as a terrifying creature slowly rose out of the centre of the pool. It was a sea monster – or at least a fierce warrior dressed as one. He was tall, broad and muscular, and his gleaming helmet was fashioned in the shape of a grotesque shark's head, mouth gaping to reveal his own savage face within. His enormous chest heaved under a breastplate of armoured scales. His forearms, each the size of a tree trunk, were encased in gauntlets studded with sharp razors, and daggers glinted from the backs of his metal boots. In his hands, each the size of Jake's head, he grasped a broadsword and a trident.

Jake's heart was now pumping at double speed. His stomach had turned to liquid. 'What is he going to do to her?' he said through clenched teeth.

'It's just a show,' Nathan tried to reassure him. 'Dreadful as she is, Agata Zeldt wouldn't put her

own daughter in any *real* danger.' Even as he spoke the words, he did not entirely believe them. The depravity of the Zeldt family had never ceased to amaze him.

The music reached a thunderous crescendo. The 'sea monster' rose until his feet were level with the surface of the water; then he stepped onto the edge of the pool and pumped his arms above his head. The music stopped dead and he let out a war cry of such ferocity that Jake had to cover his ears. Then he turned to the figure of the nymph and waited, chest heaving, for battle to commence.

All eyes swivelled to the motionless Topaz. Slowly she awoke, moving first an arm, then a leg, then lifting her head. Gradually she rose to her feet. Jake now spotted the sword at her side, which she brandished aloft, with a battle cry to challenge the monster's.

The audience cheered and leaped up in delight. Even the slaves had stopped to steal a glance at the entertainment.

'It's Andromeda and the sea monster,' Charlie said, as if in a dream.

'Who?' Jake asked, both appalled and mesmerized.

'The legend goes that her mother, Cassiopeia,

the queen of Ethiopia, bragged that she was more beautiful than Poseidon's own daughters. In revenge, the sea god let loose a terrible monster, Cetus, to lay waste to the coastline. He would stop only if Andromeda was sacrificed. So she was chained to a rock and abandoned.'

'And what happened to her then?' Jake was clenching his fists so tightly, his knuckles were white.

'Actually' – Charlie's tone brightened – 'she was saved by the warrior Perseus, who was on his way back from finishing off the Gorgon, Medusa.'

'Not that you should get any ideas,' Nathan added quickly, keeping an eye on Jake. 'Perseus was a killing machine, not an innocent schoolboy.'

Suddenly the fighting started. Cetus's massive body lunged forward, swiping at Topaz with the broadsword. Showing lightning reactions, she parried, then kicked out at him. There was a loud crunch as her foot connected with his jaw. The audience erupted as Cetus fell back. For a second his eyes swam in his head; but then fury took hold again. He surged through the water, and a nerve-shredding duel followed – parry, riposte, parry. Steel sliced against steel; sparks flew; water sprayed onto

the crowd. Topaz was quick and nimble, her foe slow and brutish. He slashed at her feet, and she jumped nimbly down into the pool – but the chain stopped her from escaping, and yanked her back.

Jake was filled with panic as she lost her footing, tripped and fell into the water. Without hesitation, Cetus's trident came down on her. She tried to dodge it, but it grazed her shoulder. Blood dripped into the foaming pool.

'We have to stop it!' Jake exclaimed, stepping forward.

'No, Jake!' Nathan held him back. 'She's ten times more able than he. It is entertainment, that is all. This is ancient Rome, remember – nothing like the place you come from.'

Topaz and the monster had retreated, panting, gazes fixed on one another. Agata's eyes sparkled and Leopardo licked his lips in anticipation. The crowd started chanting for the battle to resume. This time Topaz lunged first, and the duel became even more desperate. Suddenly she swiped her sword at her opponent's leg. There was a screech as the blade sliced through the metal of his boots and came to a stop. As she yanked it free, she lost her footing and tumbled into the pool again. Taking advantage of

this, the monster hurled his trident at her. Topaz ducked, and it thwacked into the thigh of a passing slave. The audience fell about laughing, but Topaz was distracted. Cetus advanced on her and lifted his sword for the kill. Everyone froze in anticipation.

Suddenly Jake shoved Nathan aside and ran out, unsheathing his dagger. He hurled himself into the pool and stabbed Cetus's thigh. Neither Topaz nor the crowd could identify this new masked participant at first; the guests assumed that he was the brave Perseus come to save her, and cheered with delight. Cetus gave a deep, rasping groan and tried to swing a punch at Jake, but then dropped to his knees, blood pumping from his wound.

Jake picked himself up and went over to Topaz. 'It's me,' he panted. 'The chain' – he took hold of it – 'how do I undo it?'

'Are you mad?' Topaz shook her head in fury. 'You must leave now! You risk everything.'

He paid no attention. 'How do I undo it?' he yelled again, yanking the metal links.

In the crowd, Charlie and Nathan stood frozen in horror, the latter holding Lucius back in case he was also tempted to join the fray.

'Charlie, what now?' Nathan whispered urgently.

'I don't know,' Charlie replied in despair, nodding towards Leopardo and Agata on the other side of the stage. 'Like everyone else, they think this is part of the show.'

He was right: they were both smirking, as yet unaware of what was really going on.

'Jake!' Topaz cried as Cetus suddenly lurched to his feet again. He swung Jake round, grabbed him by the neck and started to lift him off the ground. As his immense hands tightened their grip, Jake's mask fell off and his face – now a startling red – was revealed.

As Leopardo watched, his eyes began to widen in uncertainty. Then his smile gradually faded. He knew this boy: it was that inept agent from the opera house in Stockholm. Quickly he scanned the faces in the crowd and found another he recognized: Nathan Wylder. Leopardo's lips quivered and he clenched his white teeth.

Then everything happened at once.

The audience cheered as Jake was lifted higher and higher, his legs thrashing in midair. Topaz picked up a large rock and smashed it over the monster's head. His eyes bulged, then rolled up in his head. He let go of Jake, lost consciousness and fell back into the pool.

'*Periculum!* Danger!' Leopardo yelled at the top of his voice. 'Look to the emperor,' he ordered as he pushed through the mob and jumped down into the arena, unsheathing his sword as he did so.

Suddenly there was pandemonium. The screaming guests charged for the exits. Agata Zeldt slowly rose to her feet, her face incandescent with fury.

As Leopardo bore down on Jake, Nathan jumped into the ring, landing on Cetus's chest (the unfortunate soldier was just coming round when he was knocked out again) and intercepting Leopardo's blade.

'All the vermin are here, then!' The fair-haired youth swung round to face him. 'I knew that snake couldn't be trusted.'

Then swords were crashing, twisting, slicing; faces were set, fierce with concentration. In the midst of all the mayhem, Jake couldn't help appreciating what a sensational swordsman Nathan was. At times he was a peacock, but when he truly needed to fight, he was awe-inspiring – as swift and balletic as he was savage and strong. That said, Leopardo was more than a match for him, and on this occasion he was the luckier of the two. Nathan misjudged a cut by just an inch; it was enough for

his opponent to knock him off balance, strike his hand and disarm him.

Leopardo was just preparing to finish him off when Topaz finally eased apart the weak link in the heavy chain, releasing it and hurling it into his face. There was a crack as the iron struck his teeth. Jake actually saw a chunk of white enamel fly out of his mouth and land in someone's pudding. The blow was decisive: Leopardo looked incredulous, insulted; then collapsed onto his knees and fell head first into the water.

Only now, almost paralysed with white-hot fury, did Agata act, uttering a murderous cry that made people's blood run cold. 'Stop them!' she cried, thrusting her way through the crowd towards the edge of the arena.

Without thinking, Jake rushed across to intercept her, jumping over the balustrade. 'You are a monster!' he yelled as he came face to face with her. He had no weapon, but picked up a goblet of wine from the nearest table and flung its contents into her face. There was a look of astonishment, before she lunged for Jake's neck. Now he took hold of the whole table and swung it towards her. It made contact with her jaw, and her head jolted back;

plates and glasses smashed onto the ground. Jake swung again, and this time Agata lost her footing and fell onto a pile of broken crockery and half-eaten food.

Jake was about to attack her with his bare hands when Nathan yanked him back, dragging him away. 'Enough!' he ordered. There were guards everywhere, fighting their way through the frenzied crowd to come to Agata's aid. Charlie, Topaz and Lucius joined Nathan and Jake, and they forced their way back to the other side of the arena and through the archway leading into the villa.

'This way,' said Topaz, leading them along a labyrinth of slaves' corridors and back stairways until they reached the huge vaulted kitchen. Here, amidst clouds of steam and clanking metal, lackeys were busy cleaning up after the banquet. They were too tired to challenge the intruders. Charlie resisted the alluring, mouth-watering sights and smells as Topaz guided them through.

The back door was open, and just outside stood a cart, from which a hairy man in a leather apron was unloading carcasses of meat. As he disappeared inside with half a cow across his shoulder, Nathan wasted no time in leaping up onto the vehicle.

'All aboard,' he shouted as he took hold of the reins.

The others scrambled up, Charlie reeling as he came face to face with the dead eyes of a wild boar. '*Enchanté*,' he said drily as Lucius helped Topaz up and jumped on.

By the time the butcher re-emerged from the kitchen, his cart was gone.

Nathan flicked the reins, urging the horses round to the front of the villa and nearly colliding with another platoon of guards who were pouring out of the main entrance. One long-limbed soldier managed to pull himself up onto the back of the cart, sword drawn.

'Excuse me.' Charlie politely edged Topaz out of the way and launched the wild boar at their assailant. With a resounding crack, snout met face and the man was thrown off. 'There are times,' Charlie commented, dusting his hands, 'when cruelty to animals is acceptable.'

As they flew up the road, the soldiers jumped into their own wagon and set off in pursuit.

Nathan steered the rickety butcher's cart down the hill towards the Roman Forum, the ancient wheels shaking and rattling with the strain. Their

pursuers rapidly picked up speed. Within moments, the guards were firing darts from their crossbows.

Nathan whipped the horses on, faster and faster. Too late he noticed a hole in the road ahead – there was a screech of metal and the cart took off for a moment. It landed with such a jolt that Lucius over-balanced. He reached out for Topaz, but it was too late – he was already flying off the back of the cart. Topaz gasped in horror as he rolled straight into the path of the wagon.

In unison the watching History Keepers covered their eyes as Lucius was trampled by the horses' hooves. One animal tripped over the human obstacle, and came crashing down, pulling the others with it. There was a melee of dust, of neigh-ing, of twisting necks and thrashing limbs, until finally the wagon came to a halt.

'We have to stop!' Jake shouted, peering round. He could just make out Lucius's body amidst the carnage.

'You don't get to say anything!' Nathan shouted at him. '*Never again*, do you understand?' Jake had never seen his friend so angry – he was livid with rage.

Nathan shook the reins harder and urged the

horses on down the hill. Topaz sat there, shaking with a whole range of emotions – shock, confusion, exhaustion . . . and loathing for Jake. She saw Lucius's body being dragged out of the wreckage, before the cart rounded a corner and she lost sight of him.

Jake was overcome with shame. The sense of his own disgrace was so unbearable that he felt physically sick. Once again – and more catastrophically than ever – he had ruined everything.

17 Lucius Down

'Sh-sh-should we go back for him?' Jake stammered in the gloom. They had just got back to the bureau and Charlie was lighting candles, with Mr Drake sitting stiffly on his shoulder.

Nathan turned on Jake. 'I told you to keep out of this!' he said. Half an hour had passed since they escaped Agata's villa, but he was still furious. 'Do you understand?'

Jake nodded obediently.

'Your weapon, please,' Nathan demanded, sounding like a cross teacher. Jake undid his belt, fumbling clumsily with the buckle before finally releasing it. Nathan snatched the belt and scabbard from him and placed it on the table. Receiving the special sword from Nathan himself on the pier at Point Zero had been one of Jake's proudest

moments. Since then everything had turned sour. 'Now sit down over there and keep quiet!' the American ordered coldly, pointing to Jake's bunk.

He turned, headed across the room and sat down. At any moment, he knew, tears would start welling up, so he sank back into the shadows against the wall and used what little will power he had left to keep them at bay. Crying now would be the ultimate disgrace and he was determined not to let it happen.

The others did not even look at him. They went about their business: Nathan examining papers; Topaz attending to the cuts on her face in the mirror; Charlie lighting more candles. The air was thick with tension. Only Mr Drake briefly peeked over his master's shoulder to examine the malefactor in the corner. Jake looked up at him, hoping that he still had one friend, but the parrot fluffed up his feathers and turned away.

The taut silence was eventually broken by Nathan. 'The capture of Lucius Titus is regrettable,' he said matter-of-factly, 'but there will be no rescue mission. It is too dangerous and the chances are' – he bit his lip – 'the chances are he has not made it.'

Jake felt his stomach flip over. He looked at

Topaz in the mirror. She froze, her eyes flickering, but said nothing.

'Does everyone agree?' Nathan asked quietly.

It was a while before Topaz, without turning round, nodded back at him. Charlie, who had waited to hear her opinion, solemnly followed suit. Nathan bowed his head respectfully. 'As I said, it's regrettable. He was a good soldier.'

Jake had to clench his fists and take deep breaths to stop himself from leaping up and shouting that of course they should try and save Lucius; that he was sure to be alive! But he knew it was no good. The damage had been done and he was to blame for everything.

Nathan continued in a businesslike way, 'Regarding Agata Zeldt's *end of dominions* – what we know, or seem to know, is as follows. Something is going to happen during the games at the Circus Maximus tomorrow. Though the details are sketchy, it is likely to be an assassination attempt. We believe that the target is the fake Tiberius. It is possible that rebel slaves will then be blamed for his murder. Unrest will follow, and Agata will use the confusion and bloodshed as an opportunity to take control. Her master plan, her ultimate aim – and we have no

idea how she is to accomplish it – is to assume command of the Roman army. Need I tell anyone what that could lead to?' Nathan didn't wait for an answer. 'The greatest military forces the world has ever known in the hands of one of history's most demented malefactors.'

'And what exactly is she planning to do with the army?' Charlie asked, uncertain of everything.

'I don't know.' Nathan shrugged. 'Re-draw the boundaries of the world in her own diabolical image? The end of dominions, remember?'

Charlie was still shaking his head. 'It still doesn't add up,' he said. 'As a plan, it's completely flawed.' He pushed his glasses up his nose as he started to explain. 'The emperor is without doubt the supreme head of state – in fact, never has one man, in all history, held so much power. And, yes, his assassination, in full public view, by supposed rebel factions, would be catastrophic. But even then Agata couldn't take command of the army without the full support of the Senate. And this is not forgetting that the *real* Tiberius will still exist.'

'I don't know about the real Tiberius,' Nathan replied. 'Maybe he's dead already. But regarding the senate, we can only assume that she *has* their

support. Remember, she's richer than anyone in the empire . . .'

'Sure, and of course money talks, without a doubt, especially in this city,' Charlie reflected, 'but there's six hundred of them, Nathan, and the Romans are also famous for their sense of honour.'

'Then we must assume that somehow she has taken those facts into account as well,' Nathan said firmly. 'There seem be no limits to what she can do. Besides, what else do we have to go on? Our mission is clear: tomorrow morning we head for the Circus Maximus and stop this assassination from taking place.'

Although Charlie was still far from convinced, he had no option but to nod in agreement.

The mood didn't improve much after that. Jake remained sitting on his bed. Charlie rustled up a cheese board (he was ravenous, having eaten hardly anything at Agata's banquet), then the three of them sat around the table, examining a map of the Circus Maximus and discussing their plan of action. Jake watched them from the shadows, hearing only snippets of conversation: 'The emperor's enclosure is this structure here . . . The games always start

with a procession . . .' None of them turned round or spoke to him. They didn't even offer him anything to eat. He wondered if they would ever talk to him again.

Eventually Nathan rolled up the map. He stood up and gave Topaz a big hug and Jake heard him whisper, 'I'm always here for you. Always.' He turned to Charlie and gave him a warm pat on the back. 'There is one silver lining to all this, old friend,' he said. 'As our cover has been blown, we'll need to go incognito. I trust you packed your special equipment?'

'Beards and moustaches?' the other replied eagerly, producing a small case from his belt. 'I never travel without them!'

Nathan headed, yawning, towards his bed. Charlie went to sit on his bunk, gave Mr Drake a goodnight peanut and a little peck on his head, then lay down.

Jake watched Topaz as she extinguished all the candles but one on the table. Finally she put the last of the food on a plate and brought it over to Jake.

'Here,' she said, handing it to him. There were a couple of slices of cheese and some bread and pickles.

'Thank you,' he said quietly, putting it down on

the bed. 'T-Topaz,' he stammered, 'I don't even know where to begin with saying sorry. And I understand I may never be forgiven . . .' He looked up at her, blinking his big brown eyes. Her expression was cold and unsmiling, but he soldiered on. 'But, you know, I think Lucius may have a chance. He is so brave and clever and I'm sure that—'

'*Tu comprends comme sa vie a été dûr?*' Topaz interrupted him, the words almost sticking in her throat. 'Do you know how hard his life has been? Do you know what pain he has suffered?'

Jake remembered that Lucius had told him something of his life, the night they spent together on the bridge. 'He said he hadn't seen his parents since he was ten.'

'And do you know why?'

Jake shook his head.

'Because when he was ten, pirates boarded his parents' ship and took them away. His family was not rich – his father had a small boat-repair yard – but they were happy. Lucius was loved,' she said pointedly. 'One day they were sailing to Dalmatia: they'd saved enough money to build a little house there, by the sea. But just three leagues away from

the coast the pirates attacked. Lucius was brave even then and put up a fight' – a smile briefly flickered on Topaz's face – '*mais c'était inutile* – it was pointless. He was a child. He was bound, chained and separated from his father, his mother and his little brother. He never heard of them again.'

'Brother?' Jake said softly. 'He didn't tell me he had a brother.'

'They took Lucius to the nearest port and sold him in the market for two pieces of gold. He spent five years – *la reste de son enfance* – underground in a silver mine, haunted by the screams of his brother as he was carried away that day.'

Jake's insides froze with pity. He looked at Topaz and saw that her eyes were glistening. He stood up and took her hand. She did not react, but nor did she pull it away. She carried on with her story. 'Then, when I was imprisoned by my own mother, he helped me whenever he could, without a care for his own safety.' Tears streamed down her face now. 'He was a beautiful person,' she sobbed quietly. '*Un gars magnifique.*' Charlie peered over at the sorry scene, but said nothing.

Jake wanted to throw his arms around Topaz, but she quickly wiped away her tears and climbed onto

her bunk. Jake watched as she pulled up the bed-clothes and, still sobbing, turned her back on him.

Helplessly, Jake stood staring at Topaz's back. He wanted to tell her that everything would be all right; but he couldn't. The truth was, things were far from all right. Lucius was gone. And, on top of that, Agata Zeldt, the most evil woman in history, was at large. The following day she was planning an atrocity that would herald the *end of dominions*; but none of them even understood what it was, let alone how they could stop it.

At length Jake sighed and lay down on his bed. Still fully dressed, he pulled the blanket over him and stared at the wall in shame.

18 THE SECRET ROOM

'She's definitely gone,' said Alan, his binoculars trained on the retreating boat. It was dawn on the Mont St Michel, and he and Miriam were on the blustery battlements, suppressing early morning yawns.

They had waited two days for Oceane to leave her suite long enough for them to investigate the book with the palm tree on its cover. Oceane had announced the night before that she was planning a trip to the mainland to look at fabrics for her wedding. Alan and Miriam had got up at four and waited patiently, sharing a flask of coffee and watching the sea birds, until she and her pet lioness finally boarded the ferry boat (the History Keepers usually sent one daily to the mainland to pick up provisions) and departed.

'Let's go,' Miriam announced, heading for the nearest staircase. 'My toes are frozen solid.'

They made their way to Oceane's luxurious suite, slipped inside and went straight over to the pink china pot on the mantelshelf, where Oceane had put the key to the secret compartment. They had wondered if she might take it with her, so it was a great relief when they heard it clinking in the bottom. They took it out and opened up the safe behind the painting. The book with the palm tree on it was there.

Miriam seized it and examined the cover, screwing up her face in bewilderment. '*Flora of the South China Seas, 700 to 1500*,' she read blankly. 'It doesn't sound very important.' She shrugged. 'Unless of course you happen to live in the South China Seas in that time. And you're in the gardening business.'

Alan took it from her, unclasped the latch and opened it. His face lit up. 'Well, that's a little more interesting,' he said. Inside, cut into the pages, was a cavity with *another* key – this one much larger, and gold. He carefully took it out and examined it. There were curious interlocking symbols inscribed on the bow. 'Looks like Chinese. Mean anything to you?' He passed it to Miriam.

She shrugged. 'As you know, eastern languages are not my strong suit, nor yours. Galliana would know, of course. But what on earth is the key for?' She took the book from Alan and peered at the spine. 'They have volumes just like this in the archives. There must be a connection – that's where Jake saw her.'

Without further discussion they took the book and the key and made their way up stairs and down corridors, through the stateroom, then doubling back down more steps until they finally reached the intelligence section. Two decoders were already working at Meslith terminals by the light of flicker-ing candelabras. Miriam and Alan nodded good morning and went straight into the archive room. It was still gloomy, with just a glimmer of early morn-ing light filtering through the windows.

'Now let's see . . .' said Miriam, squinting along the various section headings. '*Weather, Tides, Moonrises* . . . Here we are: *Flora and Fauna*.' She leaned down and started looking carefully at the sub-headings: '*Flora . . . Mediterranean, Northern European, American, South American, Australasian, Chinese . . . South China Seas*.' She was now on her knees, examining the spine of each volume on the

bottom shelf. 'Interesting. This is where Oceane's book should be. You see – there's 700 AD, and then it goes straight to 1500 AD.' Excited now, she started pulling all the books off the shelf. Suddenly she stopped dead and gasped, 'There it is – look!'

Alan gingerly got down, peered under the shelf and saw a keyhole mounted within a golden frame. 'Shall I do the honours?' he said, producing the key and inserting it in the lock.

'This is thrilling, isn't it?' Miriam exclaimed, clutching her husband's shoulder. 'I love a secret keyhole!'

Alan turned the key easily. The lock clicked and a section of bookcase opened, revealing a low doorway that led down into a small dark space.

'A secret room!' Miriam exclaimed. 'Even better than a secret keyhole. Light – we need light. Hold on,' she said and, almost sliding along the parquet floor, dashed back to the communications room. She returned a moment later with a candelabra, taking care not to extinguish the candles. She held it up as they both stepped down into the chamber.

'Good heavens, what is all this?' Miriam gazed around in astonishment. It was a windowless cubicle, only just large enough to accommodate a

small desk, a chair and a rickety book shelf with a globe on it. On the desk lay an old Meslith machine and bundles of files stuffed with documents. The walls were covered in maps and plans. 'That's China . . .' She peered at an ancient nautical chart.

'And this is old Canton,' said Alan, inspecting another.

'They're *all* Chinese . . .' Miriam shook her head in bafflement. 'The books too; even the globe has Chinese writing on it,' she said. 'Alan, what on earth does Oceane Noire have to do with the Chinese?'

'Not just Oceane,' he remarked, picking up one of the files from the desk. 'That's Jupitus's handwriting, no question.' He showed Miriam the front of the file. In neat curling letters it was inscribed with the words:

Correspondence
Operation Black Lotus
Top Secret

He opened it up. It was full of slips of parchment – Meslith communications, all written in a distinctive Chinese alphabet. 'These are recent,' he said.

'Alan . . .' gasped Miriam, clutching her neck. 'The initials at the bottom . . .' Each of the messages was signed with the letters XIX.

'Xi Xiang?' said Alan. 'It can't be!'

They both knew the name. Just as the Zeldt dynasty terrorized the *western* world, so Xi Xiang was the History Keepers' most feared enemy in the *east*. A killer as eccentric as he was ruthless, he loved to perform, to assume disguises, sometimes dressing up as one of his slaves, sometimes wearing elaborate costumes to oversee his bloody atrocities. Of course, disguising himself was something of a joke, as Xi Xiang's face was unmistakable – he had three eyes; the third, misshapen and lazy, hung over his right temple.

'We'd better fetch Galliana,' said Miriam.

The commander came down to the archive room in her dressing gown, pale with anxiety. She inspected the secret cubicle, before removing the file and sitting down at one of the library desks. She put on her glasses and, after verifying that the handwriting on the front did indeed belong to Jupitus, opened up the file. She had barely started to scan the first line of writing before the colour leached from her

face. She clasped her hands together in horror, then leafed through the pages, eyes darting backwards and forward, until finally she slammed the file shut. Her hands shook as she removed her glasses.

'Contact Rose Djones immediately,' Galliana muttered shakily. 'She must apprehend Jupitus Cole – chain him up, whatever it takes – until he can be brought back to Point Zero for questioning.' She looked up at Miriam and Alan. Neither of them could remember seeing her look so anxious. 'Lives are at risk. Do you understand? *All* our lives!'

Three hours after his talk with Topaz, Jake still hadn't managed to sleep. A host of dreadful images spiralled around in his head – the fight in Agata's villa, Lucius's capture, Nathan's anger, Topaz's despair.

He was haunted by thoughts of young Lucius and his poor family: pirates cruelly separating them; Lucius toiling in the silver mine; the cries of his little brother fading across the sea . . . 'His brother!' Jake murmured to himself. 'Why did he not tell me he had a brother?'

And finally, on top of all this, Jake was aware that this was his *second* disaster in as many weeks. He'd

already been responsible for losing vital atomium supplies and putting the whole service in jeopardy.

He shook his head again and again, as if that might somehow banish his thoughts. It didn't work. He turned from side to side, from his front to his back; he tried to focus on the single flickering candle on the table; he took long deep breaths; he even tried counting sheep. Nothing worked: there was no peace to be found.

Finally a single idea started to emerge. It was a terrifying one – but once it had taken hold, Jake knew there was no way of getting away from it.

I will go back and find Lucius. I will find him and I will save him.

Again Jake shook his head. He turned onto his stomach and buried his head in his pillow. But he could not dispel the notion.

I can't make things worse than they already are, he nagged at himself. *Even if Lucius is already dead, at least I will have tried.* He sat up. *If anyone sees me, I will say I am going for a walk.* And before he knew it, he was on his feet and tiptoeing across the room. There were quills, ink and paper on the table. He wrote a note, folded it carefully and left it lying there. Then, gingerly, he picked up his sword and

belt from the pile of weapons and crept towards the exit.

No one woke up. Nathan was wearing his silk eye mask, smiling and mumbling to himself as he dreamed of some adventure. Charlie and Topaz were completely still. Jake quietly unbolted the door and slipped out. As it closed behind him, the candle on the table flickered and went out.

Jake fastened his belt and ran up the dark spiral staircase, past the faded mosaics. At the top, he edged open the secret door into the Basilica Aemilia. A few people lay sleeping in shadowy corners, and a handful of tradesmen were setting off on their early morning business. A hazy dawn light filtered in through the high arches as Jake stepped down into the Forum Romanum.

This too was almost deserted. The last of the night was lifting, like a grey curtain, to reveal a soft golden glow beyond. Jake saw two men on their knees, scrubbing the steps of the Senate House; a supervisor watched them, rubbing the sleep from his eyes. A figure in a white toga – a lawyer, Jake fancied – dictated a letter to his assistant as he hurried across the square, his leather sandals clicking on the stone. Three ladies flitted under the

arches of the basilica opposite. Other than that, there was not a soul to be seen.

Despite the heavy task that confronted him, Jake found himself stopping for a moment and gazing in wonder. Bathed in an otherworldly light, the place looked more splendid than ever, its colonnades of white marble even more striking. 'What a marvellous place . . . what a marvellous world,' Jake whispered to himself. Then he turned grimly in the direction of the Palatine – a steep hill covered in lavish villas interspersed with dark green cypresses. He stopped and drew a steadying breath. Although he could not see it from here, he knew that at the summit lay Agata's stronghold and his own date with destiny. He straightened his belt, squared his shoulders and set off.

He skirted around the temple of Vesta and started to weave his way up the winding slope. He was a third of the way to the top, cutting between the high walls of two immense villas, when he realized that someone was following him.

He could hear crunching footsteps; even heavy panting. His follower was not very subtle: when Jake stopped and glanced round, he threw himself clumsily behind a bush, stifling a yell on discovering

that it was covered in thorns. Jake saw him tussling with the undergrowth.

He feigned ignorance and carried on up a flight of steps, before darting into the shadow of a doorway and drawing his sword. His pursuer soon came into view. Jake could see that it was definitely a man – or a short, tubby boy, at any rate – but his face was obscured by the hood of his cape. He was wheezing, turning this way and that, mystified by the disappearance of his prey. There was something oddly familiar about him, Jake thought.

He waited until the boy had drawn level, then reached out, grabbed him and yanked him back into his hiding place, holding his sword to the boy's throat.

'Don't kill me! Please don't kill me,' the boy exclaimed, pudgy hands flapping wildly. 'Jake, it's me.'

Jake recognized the voice, but still couldn't place it. He tugged off the hood and swung the boy round. His jaw dropped in disbelief. He was about Jake's age, as wide as he was short, with ruddy cheeks, a runny nose and crazy fair hair.

'It's me, Caspar Isaksen.' The boy smiled uncertainly, then sneezed – a high, whistling sneeze.

He held up his hand and sneezed again; and a third time, the noise echoing across the valley. Then he produced a well-used handkerchief from inside his toga and started blowing his nose like a foghorn. 'So sorry,' he excused himself. 'The pollen here is truly murderous – plays havoc with my sinuses.'

'Caspar Isaksen . . .' Jake repeated, dumb-founded. It was the boy he had met the night he had lost the atomium. In fact, Caspar had borne the brunt of the disaster – shot by Leopardo and nearly drowned in the freezing Baltic. Jake had not forgotten the boy's furious tirade.

Whatever your name is, he had said, *I neither remember nor care – feel bad . . . feel like a traitor – because that's what you are.*

And here he was again – Caspar Isaksen the Third, in ancient Rome, dressed in a toga, cape and sandals, with his unruly blond hair, his cheeks ruddier than ever.

'Wh-wh-what are you doing here?' Jake stammered.

'Good question.' Caspar nodded. 'Crazy, isn't it?' Then he leaned closer and whispered, 'I appear to be on an assignment – a top-secret mission.'

'A mission?' Jake whispered back. 'What mission?'

'Hold on a minute . . .' Caspar starting fishing around in a linen sack he had thrown over his shoulder. 'I just need to check that my sesame sponge cakes are still intact – that was quite a move you sprang on me.' He withdrew a small cake from his bag, examined it briefly, then stuffed it into his mouth. 'Mmm, delicious,' he spluttered. 'These could almost make it into my top ten pastries of all time.' He thought carefully as he swallowed the last mouthful. 'Well, certainly the top twenty. Care for one?' he added, offering the bag to Jake.

He shook his head. 'I'm dying to know what you're doing here. Did Point Zero send you?'

'Of course, of course.' The boy nodded. 'Commander Goethe signed the order herself. In fact, only she and my father know about it.'

Jake remembered that Caspar's father – Caspar *Jakob* Isaksen – was in charge of all atomium production in his secret laboratory in northern Sweden. He recollected also that the Isaksen family had been the sole producers of the precious liquid since the History Keepers were first founded centuries ago.

'But what is your mission?' Jake persisted.

'As I said, it's top secret – *stratospherically* so – but

I don't suppose there is any harm in telling you. I was told that I might bump into some of you here.' Caspar looked up and down the deserted street and ushered Jake deeper into the shadow of the doorway, before continuing, 'I've been sent to try and reclaim the atomium consignment that was lost in Stockholm. Obviously you, more than anyone, will remember that . . .' he added pointedly.

Jake nodded grimly. 'And, once again, I am so, so sorry,' he replied with the utmost sincerity, 'for putting you in danger; for putting *everyone* in danger.' He was painfully aware that, during these last two weeks, he had been called on to apologize more than ever before in his life.

'Oh, let's not worry about that now,' Caspar reassured him with a pat on the shoulder. 'It's all in the past. You just did what you thought was right. Anyway, back to my mission. It turned out that the stolen atomium was fitted with some kind of tracking device. You see, each batch gives off a specific magnetic aura or something – it's all quite scientific and complicated – and Papa eventually tracked it down to these time and place coordinates, and I was sent here. I was just strolling around the Forum Romanum, wondering where I should go next,

when I saw you walking past. I didn't know if I should speak to you or not.'

Jake exclaimed excitedly, 'Well, I know where the atomium must be! I know exactly. The man who stole it from us – *the Leopard*, as he called himself then – is in a villa half a mile up this hill.'

'Really?'

'No doubt about it! We have been there already and I am on my way back.' Jake remembered the mission he had set himself, and added seriously, 'But if we are to search for the atomium, the others should certainly come with us. They are in the Roman bureau, beneath the Basilica Aemilia.'

'Where did you say it was?' Caspar asked.

'In the Forum Romanum' – Jake pointed back behind him – 'underneath the Basilica Aemilia. It's accessed through a secret door at the back of the building . . . Caspar, are you all right?'

His companion's expression had completely changed. His uncertain smile had been replaced by a sullen scowl. 'You can shut up now, Jake Djones,' he sneered.

'What?'

'You really are spectacularly idiotic. But of course, I knew that the first time I met you.' Jake

gaped in astonishment. 'You actually thought it was a coincidence, us bumping into each other?' Caspar let out a high-pitched giggle. 'I have to laugh! I made you think that *you* were the traitor in Sweden. And all the time it was me. Although that fool Leopardo wasn't supposed to actually fire a shot.'

'What are you talking about?'

Smirking, Caspar produced a thick silver bracelet from his bag – the same poison bangle worn by the Hydra. Jake stepped back in confusion.

'Stupid, stupid, stupid!' Caspar teased, advancing towards him. 'As stupid as your brother.'

'My brother?! What do you know about my brother?'

Caspar twisted the cap of the container, releasing the noxious vapour.

Jake held his hand to his mouth but it was too late – he had already inhaled the acrid smoke. It burned the back of his throat. He prayed that the vinegar he had drunk last night would still be working – but it was too long ago. *It lasts maybe three hours* – that was what Lucius had said. Instantly his insides were churning, and sharp pain shot from his skull down the length of his spine. Numbness spread from his neck to his chest, to his arms and

fingers, then to his legs and feet. He reached for his sword, but was too weak to even grasp it. As he fell forward onto his knees, Caspar put his fingers to his mouth and gave a piercing whistle. Immediately eight Hydra guards came marching towards them.

'Why?' was all Jake could say as he collapsed on the ground. He twisted onto his side, but the poison was now affecting his vision. He was vaguely aware of Caspar chuckling to himself, 'Stupid, stupid, stupid,' as he devoured another of his cakes. Then everything went black. Jake heard boots marching towards him and felt rough hands hauling him up.

And then he lost consciousness completely.

19 THE END OF DOMINIONS

'*Cruelty*, *cataclysm* . . . and *carnage* are my three favourite words,' a rich, throaty female voice announced.

'They are not just your favourite *words*, Mother,' another voice – a male one – responded. 'They are your favourite *things*.'

The first speaker acknowledged this with a laugh. 'You're quite right, my darling, as always.'

'I prefer the word *decapitation*,' a third, much younger voice added. 'It has a beautifully final ring to it.'

Jake heard this conversation as if in a dream; the voices seemed both distant and close by. He still couldn't see, but he could *feel* a number of things. His whole body throbbed with pain; his head in particular felt as if a vice were clamped around it.

He could tell from the echo of the voices that he was now in a large room; he smelled something rich and pungent. He was sitting in a chair, his hands manacled behind his back – he could feel cold hard metal digging into his wrists. He tried to move them, but this brought another wave of agonizing pain.

'Look – he's awake,' the third voice remarked. Jake now recognized it as Caspar's. 'Do we need to do anything?'

'Don't worry, he's not going anywhere,' the second speaker replied.

Jake identified him too – his slight accent was unmistakable. *Leopardo*, he said to himself . . . *Caspar*.

Jake searched for answers in the fog of his mind. His memories were all disjointed, but at length he recalled what had happened in the dark doorway on the Palatine. The young Swede had turned against him. *I made you think that you were the traitor in Sweden*, he had said, giggling, *and all the time it was me*. Jake now understood that Caspar had been working for Agata Zeldt all along; the fat, clumsy boy, from one of the most important and ancient families of the History Keepers' Secret Service – the

last person anyone would have suspected . . . *he* had betrayed them all.

Caspar had also mentioned Jake's brother. Why? What did he know? Had he seen him?

Gradually Jake's sight started to return: a dim shifting light slowly coalesced into hazy shapes. These in turn shimmered into focus. He was sitting at a long table – a vast slab of white marble. At the far end sat Agata Zeldt, with a falcon on her shoulder, Leopardo and Caspar on either side. With their pink cheeks and fair hair, the boys looked like diabolical cherubs adorning their dread queen.

On Jake's right, large windows opened out onto a tropical garden filled with oversized plants. To his left stood a long console table, also in white marble; upon it lay a series of strange-looking objects.

Set out before Jake's captors was a steaming platter of food that accounted for the pungent smell – a pile of dark, plump shapes. As Leopardo reached over and took one, Jake realized that it had a head and a long tail that stuck out stiffly. It was a mouse – or, worse still, a rat. Leopardo opened his mouth to take a bite, and Jake saw that one of his front teeth was missing, knocked out by Nathan the night before. Having bitten off the head, the boy began to

chew on the little bones. On Caspar's plate there were already four dismembered carcasses and he was devouring a fifth. Meanwhile Agata was delicately slicing a peach; her pet falcon sat perfectly still, claws gently flexing, eyes fixed on the plate of fried rodents. Agata was dressed simply in a black tunic that emphasized the pallor of her face and the red of her hair. She studied Jake for a long time before she spoke.

'The History Keepers are certainly letting things slide,' she whispered with a sneer, 'if *you're* the sort of agent they are producing these days. I've seen fiercer-looking sand-flies.'

This elicited a snigger from Leopardo and a high-pitched giggle from his partner in crime. Jake turned to Caspar in fury, but when he opened his mouth to curse him, he found that it was still numb. Incoherent sounds emerged, along with a spray of spittle, and Caspar once again fell about laughing.

A battle between Jake and his facial muscles finally resulted in words: 'Your f-father,' he stammered. 'He's a t-traitor too?' He was determined, first of all, to establish how deep the conspiracy went.

Immediately Caspar's smile soured. 'My father is stupid!' he hissed. 'A stupid old man who treats me like a child. Why do you think I am here?'

'You – you *are* a child,' Jake managed. 'A spoiled, good-for-nothing child.' Each word was agony – his throat felt like sandpaper – but he continued doggedly, 'Where is Lucius?'

It was Leopardo's turn to be amused. 'That brainless hunk? You'll find out soon enough.'

'That's right.' Caspar gulped down another mouthful and wiped his greasy mouth on his sleeve. 'In no time at all, you'll be dying together.'

Despite everything, Jake couldn't help feeling a pulse of relief on hearing that Lucius was still alive; it meant that the claim he had made to Topaz was at least partly true. 'I would rather *die* with him than *eat* with you,' he spat.

'Oh, don't worry,' Caspar retorted, sniggering. 'You won't be eating . . . you'll be *eaten*.'

Jake ignored him and turned his attention to Agata. 'And you are worse than your brother. Ten times worse.'

Leopardo turned to his mother to gauge her reaction, but she was smiling. 'Rare praise indeed,' she purred as she put a dripping slice of peach into

her mouth. 'Of course, I always knew that Xander was just an amateur.'

'Worse than him,' Jake continued, 'because what you are doing is so completely pointless.'

Now Agata's smile faltered. In the same instant, her falcon quickly turned to Jake, its beak opening.

'Pointless!' Jake repeated firmly. Had he not been pushed to the limit in the last twenty-four hours, had he not been told that he was about to die, perhaps he would not have spoken in this way. But he wanted to get under Agata's skin – and knew he could do that by piquing her sense of rivalry with her brother. 'At least Xander had a vision. You have nothing.'

Now Agata's face turned to thunder. 'I have a vision' – she thumped the table – 'you ill-mannered upstart!' Her falcon shrieked and flapped its wings as she got to her feet, bringing her fist down on the marble again. 'I have more vision than *anyone*. Soon I will own the world.'

Leopardo stood up, trying to calm her, but Agata pushed him aside. Her bird took wing and circled the room, crying out as she swept down the table towards Jake. He looked up as she approached, trying to look defiant, but his blood ran cold and

his hands were shaking. He could see the lattice of blue veins under the pale skin, the dangerous black eyes, the thin, bloodless lips.

'By this time tomorrow' – she leaned close, and from her mouth came the odour of decay – 'I will be the most powerful ruler the world has ever seen. A *woman* – not a man; not a vain, arrogant male . . . a *woman* will rule the world.'

Only now did Jake understand the hatred that consumed her; it was directed not just at her brother, but at all men. 'Bring him,' she hissed as she turned to the nearby table.

Leopardo came over and, grinning his gap-toothed smile, unlocked Jake's manacles, yanked him to his feet and dragged him towards Agata. Jake's legs were still numb from the poison and he could barely stand.

'Do you know what this is?' Agata asked, pointing to the first object on the table. Close up, Jake recognized it immediately: it was a replica of the Circus Maximus, larger than the miniature one he had seen in the campaign room, a beautifully rendered architect's maquette. He did not reply.

'It is the greatest stadium that the world has ever known.' Agata clasped her long fingers around the

model. 'An exquisite construction, don't you think?' She pointed to the *pulvinar*, the royal box that Charlie had pointed out the night before. 'This is where I shall sit with the emperor to watch the *entertainment.*'

'Entertainment!' Caspar giggled at Agata's choice of word.

'I will watch the senators and generals taking their places,' she said, tapping her fingers along the *spina*, the stone island in the centre of the arena. 'I will watch them all, Rome's most eminent citizens – those six hundred *men* who rule the world. I will watch them as they gather for the big race. They, like everyone at the Circus Maximus, will expect excitement, drama . . . maybe some death . . .' Agata's voice sank to a whisper. 'They won't be disappointed.'

'No, they won't be disappointed at all,' Caspar agreed, panting with anticipation. Jake was sickened.

'And *this* is the device that will *guarantee* all this – all that excitement and drama and death.' Agata whistled through her teeth as she pointed to the next object on the table. Jake recognized this one too: a curious container made of thick glass,

hexagonal in shape and filled with black powder. Jake had seen a number of identical receptacles in the laboratory in Vulcano, but this one was studded with a network of minute pipes and cogs.

'This is the spare, of course, the prototype,' Agata told him, 'which I shall keep for posterity. The rest were installed in the Circus Maximus last night. Look,' she said, amused by the expression on Jake's face, 'he doesn't even know what it is.' She pinched his chin between her bony fingers. 'It's gunpowder, stupid. That ingenious combination of sulphur, charcoal and potassium – though of course we have spiced it up with some of our own special ingredients. Naturally, if you know your history, we *should* have to wait a thousand years to see it: the first batch is due to explode in 1044 AD. But it is such a delicious invention, it seems a shame to make people wait.'

Caspar listened, agog, and stuffed another mouse into his mouth, crunching the bones.

'And what better place to unveil it,' Agata went on, 'what finer location to introduce *modern carnage* to the ancient world, than the greatest and largest stadium of all time' – her eyes sparkled with fire – 'with a hundred and fifty thousand people watching?'

Jake was beginning to put the pieces together. In Vulcano, they had also discovered sulphur mines and reserves of charcoal. Now he understood why. 'You're going to blow up the Circus Maximus?' he found himself asking.

'Don't be dull-witted,' Agata replied. 'That would be pointless. There would be no one left to enjoy it!' She shrieked with laughter, and Leopardo and Caspar joined in. 'No, no, no. We shall be obliterating only a *very* select few.' She returned to the model of the Circus Maximus and pointed to the *spina*. 'Just the people here . . .' Her eyes bored into Jake's. 'Here, at the climax of the race, as the seven turns . . .'

As the seven turns . . . Jake noted the expression, but still didn't understand it.

'As the seven turns, *a fireball*, the like of which the world has never seen, will herald the bloodiest revolution of all time.'

'The senators?' Jake gasped to himself.

'All massacred. The leaders of this stagnant empire burned to dust!'

'And those who are not burned,' Leopardo added, 'will fall into the animal pits below and be torn to pieces.'

'What. Spectacular. Entertainment!' Agata cried out loud. Caspar clapped his hands in delight.

Agata's tone became playful again. 'Everyone dies – except one. Our emperor will be saved – not the real one, of course; he will be slaughtered on Capri – I already control all lines of communication to him. And Sejanus too will meet an unpleasant end. No, my *puppet* emperor. Following this catastrophe, "Tiberius" will announce his *permanent* return to Rome, to his people. He alone will command the great Roman legions – the greatest army in the world – against the "rebel factions", the "slave uprising" responsible for the bloodshed.'

She reached out and clasped her son's hands. 'For their own safety, the people will be crushed, controlled, *dominated*.' Her expression soured again. 'Before they are eradicated.'

Now Caspar hurried over and held out his chubby hands to join the other two.

Agata continued, as if in a dream, 'I will lay waste to the empire. Destroy all its literature, its libraries of knowledge. Purge its scientists and architects and planners. Demolish the bricks of civilization piece by piece, until there is nothing left but crushed bones and forgotten ideals. Then I shall own the

world, control all its riches – its gold, iron, copper, silver, salt, and the remains of its stinking masses. A woman will rule.'

Now Jake understood the extent of her master plan. Its sheer audacity was mind-blowing. Agata Zeldt did not mean to assassinate the emperor (or rather the *fake* emperor). She intended quite the opposite: to eradicate the entire government *around* him; the senators and generals who had been running the empire since Tiberius became a recluse. She then meant to use her puppet dictator, the actor Austerio – as well as her rich, greedy friends from the banquet last night – to take control. Furthermore, she would blame this act of supreme anarchy on a non-existent uprising of slaves and fan the flames of chaos even more. Gradually she would immobilize the world, steep it in fear. Then she would tear it to pieces. She would destroy, for all time, the legacy of Rome that Charlie had talked of the day they entered the city – the great systems of law and government; the education and communication; the common language, the written word, the art and architecture. These and a million other advances would all be destroyed and the world plunged into a dark age.

'Now,' Agata said, ruffling Jake's hair, 'the time has come for you to die. Bring him,' she ordered, and swept out of the room. Leopardo pushed Jake along in her wake.

She led the way up the corridor, her falcon on her shoulder. As usual, any passing slaves froze, trembling, and bowed their heads. Jake hobbled along behind her, repeatedly shoved in the back by Leopardo; the grinning Caspar brought up the rear.

A pair of ivory double doors swung open, and they entered a room that was even larger than the last. It was dominated by a giant aviary. Jake heard a deep cackle and saw, on the right-hand side of the cage, three massive, bloodthirsty vultures. Last night he had seen the room from above, as they were crossing the roofs. But he hadn't appreciated the sheer size of the birds.

As Agata approached them, cooing with delight, they flung themselves excitedly at the bars, flapping their wings and jabbing their claws at her. She let them nip at her hands, ignoring the pain and the dripping blood. Her pet falcon shrank away from them, digging its talons deeper into her shoulder.

'Put him in there!' Agata barked without turning round.

Before he knew what was happening, Jake was being dragged towards the cage. His heart thumped at double, then triple speed. He turned in desperation. 'What do you know about my brother?' he shouted at Caspar.

The boy merely sniggered as the iron grille was swung open and Jake tossed inside. He gasped as it slammed shut behind him, then turned to face the vultures, his hands raised protectively. Only when they flew up against the bars did Jake realize that he had been placed in a separate compartment — though this was no doubt a temporary reprieve. As he edged back, he tripped on something. He shuddered to find a pile of bones, stripped bare but for the odd shred of putrid flesh. He had seen this grisly cadaver from the skylight last night, but there was even less of it now. The stench made him retch and stagger back — setting Caspar off again, giggling and clapping his hands.

'Don't worry, your time will come too,' Agata said, approaching her prisoner, 'once we have returned from the Circus Maximus. By then my darlings' — she waved at the vultures — 'will be truly ravenous.'

'What do you know about my brother?' Jake persisted.

Agata ignored him and headed for the door.

He shouted after her: 'Your plan will fail. The others are ten steps ahead of you!'

Agata turned and whispered through bloodless lips, 'Caspar's right, you *are* simple. We knew the bureau was somewhere below the Forum Romanum, but had not pinpointed it. *You yourself gave us its precise location.* In about ten minutes' time your fellow agents will also be dead – those two inept boys, along with the ungrateful traitor who was once my daughter.'

Jake's fear was banished completely. 'She was never your daughter. She got close to spy on you, that's all.'

Agata bared her teeth in rage; her cheeks momentarily turned crimson. 'Prepare for death,' she warned him, then took Leopardo's arm and left the room.

'I can't wait,' Caspar jeered from the doorway. 'The lousier the agent, the tastier the lunch!' And he slammed the doors shut behind them.

Jake was alone – apart from the vultures, which stuck their necks through the bars. Their loud cries had now turned to furtive cackles, as if they were already plotting how to divide up the feast.

'You don't scare me,' Jake shouted at them. It was a lie of course – they terrified him – but it helped him a little. He rushed at them, shouting a war cry. They shot away from the bars in surprise, but returned moments later, eyeing him hungrily.

'You tell 'em, Yake,' croaked a voice from the back of the cage.

Jake's heart leaped. 'Lucius . . .?' he called into the gloom. Only now did he notice the hunched figure in the corner. As he approached, Lucius looked up and Jake did a double-take. The soldier was a shadow of his former self – caked in blood, his face covered in cuts and bruises, one eye so swollen it was almost invisible.

'What would Nathan say?' Lucius forced the glimmer of a smile as he gently touched his shiner. 'Not popping now, are they?'

Jake laughed, despite himself, knelt down and threw his arms around him.

'Ow!' Lucius cried. 'Broken rib.'

'Sorry, sorry.' Jake let go and sat down beside him. 'So great to see you . . . *almost* alive.'

Although it was clearly agony, Lucius started laughing too. Then the vultures began crashing

against the bars again, reminding them both of the fate that awaited them.

'So, Yake,' Lucius said finally. 'Six hours I plan how to get out of here.'

'Really? And . . . ?'

He shook his head. 'There is no way out. Unless you can walk through walls.'

'Oh, I see.'

Then, with a shrug, Lucius produced something from inside his tunic. 'I have this.' He passed Jake a battered silver bracelet, one of the Hydra's poisoning devices. 'I stole from a guard, but it is almost empty.'

'Well, that's a start!' said Jake, so enthusiastically that it took even him by surprise. It was a Djones family trait to be upbeat in the face of disaster. He examined the bracelet, a wrist band studded with a disc-like capsule that turned to release the gas. Very carefully, he put it to his ear and shook it. Lucius was right: there was just the tiniest amount of liquid inside.

'What about vinegar?' Jake asked. 'Do you have that?'

From the back of the device, Lucius pulled out a little vial and held it up. 'But even if we make the

birds sleep,' he said gloomily, 'we are still in the cage.'

Jake glanced once again at the pile of human remains; but Lucius reached over and turned Jake's head the other way.

Jake leaned back against the wall and closed his eyes. They were as trapped as it was possible to be: locked in a cage, sealed in a room, encased within a fortress; completely unarmed, with three of the most savage creatures on earth watching over them. Jake knew that they didn't stand a chance.

20 The Claws of Death

Topaz woke and immediately sensed that something was wrong. Nathan and Charlie were still fast asleep. She peered over the side of her bunk and realized that Jake wasn't there. She scanned the room, but there was no other sign of life.

She let herself down to the floor. Mr Drake, who had also been snoozing, perched on the end of Charlie's bunk, opened one eye and watched as she headed across the room to the door. She found the bolts undone. Mystified, she opened it, went out onto the dark landing and peered up the staircase. A warm wind blew down into her face. She was about to close it again when she suddenly heard a tapping. Someone was trying to get in from the Basilica Aemilia.

Jake, Topaz thought. *He must have locked himself*

out. She quickly ascended the steps, her bare feet silent on the stone. From the walls, Julius Caesar – depicted in mosaic, speaking in the Senate House – seemed to observe her as she flitted past. She heard a loud thump from above. Then another.

'Jake?' she called. Silence greeted her. 'Is that you?' she said more tentatively, her hand reaching out for the handle. Still no one replied. Topaz looked back down the stairs; the only sound was the faint whistling of the wind.

Suddenly there was an almighty cry, a great splintering of wood; then the door flew open and two guards burst in. Topaz gasped, turned and ran, but a huge gauntleted hand grabbed her gown. She ripped it free, but overbalanced and tumbled down the steps, banging into the mosaic wall. Again, Julius Caesar watched as she quickly picked herself up. Out of the corner of her eye, she saw several more guards, all wearing grey breastplates and beaked helmets, rushing in, weapons clanking at their side. She flew down the steps and burst through the door into the bureau.

'Hydra – here!' she cried at the top of her voice.

Nathan and Charlie had already been woken by the noise, and now leaped to their feet. As the

enemy thundered down onto the landing, Topaz slammed the door – but a metal gauntlet had managed to slide through the gap and stopped it from closing. In moments, Nathan and Charlie were at Topaz's side, pushing against the door with such force that the gauntlet began to buckle. Finally they heard a cry of pain and the arm withdrew. Nathan and Charlie quickly shot the bolts home.

Topaz took a slug from the bottle of vinegar and passed it to the others. Now the guards were pounding against the door. The two iron bolts were no match for them. Within moments, the housing of the top one was coming loose.

'We leave by the aqueduct,' Nathan shouted as he ran over to Jake's bunk. Only now did he realize that he was missing. 'Where's Jake?'

'He was gone when I woke up,' said Topaz.

'Gone?' Nathan barked. 'Where?'

'I don't know,' she snapped back, then nodded at the door. 'Shall we talk about this later?'

By now Mr Drake had flown up and was circling the room in panic. Nathan pushed the bunk to one side, clearing the area around the grille that led down into the Aqua Virgo. He took the key from its hiding place behind a loose brick in the wall,

unlocked the grille and pulled it out of its casing. It was heavy and the veins on his neck bulged with the strain. 'You first!' he called to Topaz.

But she was running around grabbing things, and already had the Meslith machine tucked under her arm. She was just collecting the bundle of weapons from the table when she noticed Jake's note. She unfolded the paper and read the one-line inscription: *I've gone to sort it out.*

'Topaz! Let's go,' Nathan shouted.

She scrunched up the note in her hand, went over to the hole and chucked the swords through. Then Charlie helped her down until she was low enough to jump, splashing into two feet of fast-flowing and surprisingly cold water. A round borehole, about as high as she was tall, disappeared off in either direction – pale, clay-like rock smoothed by decades of flowing water. She knelt down and retrieved the weapons.

Above her, the pounding on the door grew louder. The top bolt gave way and sprang across the room past Mr Drake.

'Here, quickly!' Charlie called the parrot as he too began to lower himself into the water. Mr Drake swooped down, alighted on his master's shoulder and clung on tight.

Now the second bolt sheared off, the door crashed open and the guards burst in.

Nathan followed Charlie and pulled the hatch down behind him. He produced the key and was about to turn it in the padlock when a blade shot down through the grille, only just missing his eye. The key fell, splashing into the torrent. Meanwhile Topaz had grabbed a dagger and thrust it through the grille towards the soldier – who now released a cloud of poisonous gas. It made them choke, even though they held their breaths, but had no further ill effects.

Charlie had noted exactly where the key had fallen; he plunged his hand into the water until he had located it, then thrust it into the lock. He had managed to turn it only halfway when four blades appeared above his head. The three agents jumped back to avoid them. The guards pulled at the grille – but the pressure on the padlock forced the key round and it dropped out into the water again. The gate was locked.

'Let's go!' Nathan shouted.

'There'll be an exit at the baths of Agrippa . . .' Charlie waded through the water, his voice echoing around the tunnel. 'From there it's only a short walk to the Circus Maximus.'

* * *

Jake had been sitting in the corner of the cell for half an hour, his hands covering his ears to block out the increasingly high-pitched screeches, when he suddenly noticed the glinting buckle at his waist. He realized that it didn't belong to his own plain leather belt; it was Nathan's, with its distinctive lion's head. He had been in such a state of panic when he left the bureau that he had mistakenly picked up Nathan's weapon and belt. Of course, Agata's men had taken the sword and scabbard, but mercifully had left the belt.

'Nathan, you might have saved us!' he gasped, leaping to his feet, unfastening the belt and examining the golden lion's head. He remembered Dr Chatterju demonstrating the device in the armoury at Point Zero. It contained a miniature winching mechanism that could lift a person (well, Dr Chatterju's slight nephew Amrit, at any rate) into the air.

'What's going on?' Lucius asked, looking up.

Jake was too excited to reply. He turned, strode over to the bars and, ignoring the occupants of the other cage, scanned the ceiling above it – in particular the skylight through which he had peered the night before.

'Just as I thought . . .' He clenched his fists in delight. 'The skylight's not locked. That's our exit!'

Lucius craned his neck round to see what Jake was talking about, but was none the wiser.

'So, how do we get to it, you ask . . .' Jake continued breathlessly, pacing backwards and forward, muttering. Lucius stared at him, baffled, until Jake suddenly clapped his hands together. 'It might just work.'

'What might work, Yake?'

'One of us stays in here, armed with what's left of the Hydra's gas. Let's just pray we have enough. The other opens this gate, the birds fly in, we release the gas, they collapse' – Jake, who loved a bit of acting when the occasion demanded it, threw in a mime of anesthetized vultures sinking to the ground – 'we occupy *their* chamber, closing the gate behind us, and then use Dr Chatterju's magic belt to escape!'

Jake might as well have been talking in ancient Egyptian for all Lucius could make of it. It took many minutes of patient explanation, illustrated with diagrams drawn in the sand on the floor, before he began to grasp the plan; though even then, Chatterju's miniature pulley was beyond him,

and Jake suggested that he would just have to trust him on that.

Partly because of Lucius's injuries, but mainly because Jake wanted to prove his bravery, he volunteered for the more dangerous job of vulture-bait.

They shared out the tiny flask of vinegar and took their positions – Lucius by the gate, Jake in the centre of the cell, primed with the silver bracelet. Sensing that something was afoot, the vultures started flinging themselves against the bars again.

'Remember' – Jake's firm voice masked his inner terror – 'hold your breath for at least a minute so you don't inhale the gas – I'm not sure if there was really enough vinegar to be effective.'

'And what if there is not enough gas to make them sleep?' Lucius asked.

In truth Jake was unsure about this as well: they were unarmed, and if the plan failed they would be eaten alive, the flesh ripped from their bones. But the alternative was far, far worse. 'Lucius, listen to me,' Jake said in a low voice. 'In an hour's time, in the Circus Maximus, a catastrophe is going to take place – a disaster to end all disasters. If we don't get out of here and find a way to stop it' – he took a

deep breath – 'the world *as we know it* will end today.' He snapped his fingers. '*Boom!* All gone!' It sounded dramatic, like something Nathan would say, but it was also true. Only Jake knew the details of Agata's master plan. He *had* to escape and get to the Circus Maximus – or die trying. He held up the silver bracelet and took a deep breath. 'There'll be enough, I am sure of it. Now open the gate.'

He gritted his teeth as Lucius slid the grille across to allow the birds through.

For a moment they were confused; the cawing died down and they backed away from the opening suspiciously.

'Not hungry any more?' Jake jeered.

Lucius watched the vultures as they huddled together, as if discussing their course of action. Finally their hunger took over; they turned in unison and took off, soaring through the gap.

'Now!' Jake shouted to Lucius, taking a great gulp of air before turning the capsule on the silver bracelet to release its contents. The birds flew, missile-like, towards him, their huge wings making the cage dark.

The faint red vapour billowed up from Jake's wrist, and he fought to hold his breath as the first

vulture swooped down, claws finding his neck, beak darting towards his eyes. He shielded his head with his hands as the second bird thumped down, then the third. For a moment there was a whirl of screeching and slashing, feathers and claws. Then, quite suddenly, it stopped. One vulture let out a guttural cry, and thumped to the floor. A second quickly followed. The last, the largest of the three, continued to swoop down towards Jake, staring at him defiantly, until it too was overcome and dropped onto the sand.

As Jake leaped over its sprawling body, the vulture twisted and momentarily raised its head, but collapsed onto the floor again. Jake tore through the opening into the birds' compartment. Lucius followed and they slid the gate across behind them.

It stuck halfway.

Lucius pushed with all his might, until the veins in his neck bulged, but the metal of the grille was now distorted and wouldn't slide across. He and Jake rattled it frantically, but it wouldn't budge. The opening was now maybe a foot wide. Perhaps it was enough to keep the vultures inside.

'We go back in,' Lucius suggested. 'Break their necks.'

Jake shook his head. The effects of the gas were already wearing off: he could see a wing twitching, then a leg. 'Let's go!' He stopped at a point directly below the skylight, then looked at Lucius and pointed towards a spade leaned inside the feeding bucket just outside the cage. 'Get that. We may need it.'

Lucius did as he was told, slipping his hands through the bars and retrieving the shovel. The coating of dried blood and entrails made it stick to the pail and he had to pull it loose.

Jake surveyed the barred skylight above him: it had a timber frame. In order to provide the strongest hold he would need to fire the dart deep into this. It was a small target and he only had one chance to get it right. Urgency made him bold. 'Lucius, stand in front of me,' he instructed.

Jake positioned himself behind his companion, using Lucius's shoulder to steady his hands. He held up the buckle, aimed the lion's mouth at the wooden frame, carefully pushed down on the green eye – and fired.

There was a sharp whistle, followed by a flash. Before Jake had registered it, the silver dart struck the wood with a solidly satisfying *twang*. Jake pulled

the wire tight. Dr Chatterju had boasted: *It could take the weight of Henry the Eighth – even in his heavy period*. Jake would find out very soon if this was even half true. Lucius was certainly no lightweight, and the two of them together would test the claim.

'You put the belt on,' said Jake, 'and I'll hold on to you.'

Lucius obliged, fastening it tightly around his waist. Meanwhile Jake took hold of the spade.

Suddenly they heard a clanging of metal behind them. The largest vulture had woken up and was now flying towards the bars. Still groggy, it misjudged the narrow opening and crashed down to the floor. Furious, it let out an ear-splitting screech before launching itself into the air again. *Crash!* Once more it struck the sides of the gap, but this time one wing got stuck; it struggled helplessly, then freed itself, clattering down again, the wing flapping uselessly. Unable to fly, it spat its fury. It was enough to wake its two partners in crime. Their wings stirred, their necks convulsed and their murderous eyes shot open.

'I think that's our cue,' said Jake, holding onto Lucius while tightening his grip on the spade. 'Press the blue eye. Now!'

Lucius pushed the sapphire into the lion's eye socket.

Nothing happened.

The other two vultures were getting to their feet now. One took off and flew around its new compartment, clumsily at first but gradually picking up speed. Jake realized it would be a matter of moments before it angled its way through the gap.

'Again!' Jake shouted. 'Push it again!'

Lucius pressed the button firmly. Now the line tightened, cracking like a whip, and they were quickly pulled off their feet, slowing down as their weight began to tell. Then, with a stiff click, the line stopped completely. They were just over halfway to the skylight, hanging by a straining metal thread.

'Use your hands,' Jake hissed.

Lucius reached up, and as he took hold of the line, the pressure on the buckle eased and the machine continued to ratchet them up again. They climbed inch by inch towards the skylight, Jake's knuckles whitening as he held on, Lucius's hands straining on the cord. Above them the wooden frame creaked as the silver dart pulled down on it.

They were almost within touching distance when the circling vulture managed to get the angle right

and swoop through the opening. Jake flinched as it flew up towards him. He tried to hit it with the spade, but he could only use one hand, and it was too crafty. There was a rush of air as it beat its wings, before lunging towards his neck. He felt a sharp pain, and blood started trickling down his back. Above him the metal dart shuddered. Lucius continued to pull on the wire, his hands now raw and bloody where the line had cut into them. The vulture flapped its gargantuan wings once more, this time coming in for the kill.

Jake's eyes made contact with the bird's as he swung back his weapon. The rough blade cracked into the vulture's head. For a second it seemed to freeze in midair, then it choked, its neck coiling, and spiralled lopsidedly to the ground, lurching drunkenly along the floor before shaking itself back to life.

The boys had inched upwards only a fraction before it took off again. Then the next monster, the leanest and swiftest of the three, flew in and joined its accomplice; both circled around them now.

As Lucius reached his bloodied hand up towards the bars of the skylight, the two birds launched their attack from either side. It was a terrible assault, like

treading water in a sea of daggers and razor blades. And although Jake kept his head down and eyes closed, he could feel the thump of their muscular wings and the sharp piercing of their talons.

'Yake! I can't hold,' Lucius wailed desperately. Jake opened his eye just enough to see Lucius's bloody fingers still straining on the cord as he ignored the pecks of the vultures. Above them, the silver dart was creaking and straining alarmingly.

Then Jake had a sudden thought: the silver bracelet. He still had it round his wrist. Perhaps there was a drop left inside. Even if it stopped the onslaught for a second, it would be worth it! 'Lucius, hold your breath,' he yelled as he twisted the cap. Nothing happened – there was not even the faintest whiff of gas. As he felt a beak tearing at his back, he closed his eyes. He thought again of his mum and dad – of Philip.

Suddenly he heard a booming voice; a roar so deep and guttural, it did not sound human. It was Lucius. He bellowed at the vultures, his face turning crimson. It was effective. For just a second, the birds hesitated – allowing Lucius to seize one by its neck. It shrieked, choking, beating its wings wildly. Lucius squeezed harder, teeth clenched, forcing the life out

of it, until finally it went limp and he let it fall to the floor.

The last bird attacked with renewed fury, claws raking Jake's face and seeking a purchase on his back. Jake smashed the bracelet against the ceiling to open it. As the casing fell away, a tiny crimson cloud escaped, before dissolving into the air. It was enough: the vulture breathed it in; then its claws loosened and it fell, unconscious, to the floor.

Jake looked up at Lucius, who nodded, the glimmer of a smile on his face.

Then *crack!*

The wood gave way above, the silver dart about to rip itself out. Jake felt his stomach lurch and instantly thrust the shovel up through the skylight, hooking the edge of the blade through the bars as the wire snapped free and spun away below them. Lucius, with any strength he had left, managed to grab hold of the frame, unlatch the bars, then haul himself through and pull Jake up behind him.

For a while they lay motionless on the roof, their chests heaving up and down, before Jake turned to his companion. 'We need to go. Now.'

Four hundred miles south of the city of Rome, in

the villa overlooking the port of Messina, Jupitus Cole was woken by the tip of a rusty harpoon softly digging into his cheek. He opened his eyes and peered up at Rose, who was standing over him with a face like thunder, brandishing the weapon.

'Rosalind, why are you pointing a fish hook at me?' he asked calmly.

'Because it was the first weapon I could find,' she snapped.

Jupitus examined her more carefully – her rigid stance and gritted teeth. 'I usually find a cup of tea is a better way to start the day,' he replied in his most velvety tones, moving the point away with his little finger.

'If you move so much as an inch,' she told him, 'I *will* kill you!' To make herself clear, she thrust the harpoon further into Jupitus's throat.

Jupitus made an elaborate show of freezing like a statue. 'Did I forget your birthday?' he purred.

'Operation Black Lotus – what is it?'

He chuckled. 'What?'

'Jupitus Cole, I am not joking – I will cut your throat if I have to. You are unable to walk, remember. You do not stand a chance. Operation Black Lotus,' she repeated. 'What is it?'

He stared at her and shrugged. 'I have no idea what you are talking about.'

'I just received an urgent Meslith from Galliana,' Rose continued, producing a parchment and waving it at him.

'Girl's talk?'

Rose suddenly brought the harpoon down with a thump onto the pillow, before pointing it at Jupitus's neck again. 'She's found your secret room. Yours and Oceane's little hideaway,' she spat.

Jupitus frowned, then stared up at Rose with flinty eyes. Finally he said in a quiet voice, 'It's nothing to do with Oceane. She was just picking up messages for me.'

Rose gasped, practically hyperventilating with the shock. 'So it's *true*? You are actually in cahoots with Xi Xiang?'

'It's a little more complicated than that—'

'Complicated?! There are more than a hundred communications between the two of you!' Rose was pushing the harpoon into his neck so hard, it pierced the skin. 'Xi Xiang is one of our most hated enemies. Do I need to remind you that he butchered Galliana's husband, along with her only child? That he tied weights to the boy's feet and

threw him off his ship? And you are plotting with him? You are a monster, Jupitus!'

Jupitus watched her, showing neither fear, nor anger, nor even guilt, but only the profoundest pity. He waited for her to calm down and then spoke in a soothing voice. 'Rose, listen to me. You may not believe what I tell you now, but it is the truth.' He took a deep breath. 'Yes, I have a secret room at Point Zero, from where I have communicated with Xi Xiang.'

This brought only sobs from Rose. Jupitus carried on softly, 'As you remember, Rose, Xiang and I, years ago, used to be friends.'

'Of course I remember! How could I forget?'

'But for nearly two decades we did not speak. Two years ago, a chance encounter brought us together in Tibet, in a distant corner of the Zhou dynasty. It was an extraordinary coincidence, nothing else, but I saw an opportunity and I took it.'

'What opportunity?'

'I pretended that I was disillusioned with the History Keepers, that I wanted a new life.'

'You *pretended*?'

'I became, in effect, a double agent, a *spy*, passing on "secrets" from Point Zero. Nothing important,

nothing that would affect anyone, but enough to make Xiang believe that I was on his side and take me into his confidence.'

'If you were really a double agent, why didn't you tell Galliana?'

'You know why. Galliana can think straight about everything but Xi Xiang. It is her Achilles' heel. She would have closed down the operation immediately.'

Rose shrugged, reluctantly agreeing.

'Finally my work started to pay off,' Jupitus continued. 'The Black Lotus is the name of a project Xiang has been working on for years. Even now, I have only the sketchiest details. He was about to pass on vital information when the trail suddenly went completely cold. I have heard nothing from him since I left for London months ago, and have no idea where he is or whether he is alive or dead. The day we set sail for Italy, I asked Oceane Noire to check my secret bureau twice a day, in case anything had come through.'

Rose did not take the harpoon away, but she let it drop slightly.

'And Rosalind,' Jupitus continued, looking at her very seriously, 'I have to say, it felt good to be doing

something important again. To be back in the game. It's the young ones who have all the excitement. We're nothing more than pen pushers these days.'

The phrase struck a chord with Rose. She smiled sadly and mulled over everything he had said. 'So Oceane Noire is just working for you?' she asked.

'Do you know why I proposed to Oceane?'

'I haven't the slightest idea.' Rose put her nose in the air. 'I assumed she'd put a voodoo spell on you.'

'Because she told me that if I didn't ask her to marry me, she'd tell everyone I was spying for Xi Xiang – and prove it. I'd worked too hard on the operation to give it up then.'

Rose felt another rush of emotion and tears came to her eyes. 'You – you mean,' she stammered, 'you *don't* love Oceane Noire?'

It was something that rarely happened, but Jupitus's eyes twinkled and his mouth curled into the warmest, most beautiful smile. 'Rosalind, how could you think such a thing?'

21 Circus Maximus!

'There she is,' said Charlie, peering out from the shadows. 'Isn't she just breathtaking?'

Topaz and Nathan nodded in agreement, the latter, for once, struck dumb. They were huddled in a portico in a dark corner of a long square that was packed with people. The boys were already wearing Charlie's disguises; beards and moustaches that made them look much older – in particular Nathan's, which was thick and black. Topaz had pulled her hair back and half hidden her face under the hood of her cape.

The object of their attention was the vast building at the far end of the square, towards which the crowd was hurrying.

The Circus Maximus.

They were facing its immense rear end, its

northwestern facade, and up close for the first time they could see that, even by the standards of ancient Rome, the building was a monster. Each of the two giant towers was surmounted by a striking golden statue of galloping horses and god-like charioteers, at least five times life size. The towers were connected by a series of twelve enormous arches, through which Charlie and the others could just glimpse the interior of the arena – tier upon tier of white marble, gleaming in the morning sun as the population of Rome packed themselves in.

'Can you hear it?' Nathan asked, uncharacteristically spooked. He was referring to the unearthly roar that came from within the walls – like the sound of a great wave, crashing over and over.

'That'll be a hundred and fifty thousand people taking their seats,' Charlie explained with a twinkle in his eye.

It had taken them nearly an hour to get here from the Roman bureau and their clothes were now almost dry (it was barely nine in the morning but stifling already). They had waded through the tunnel before arriving, as Charlie had predicted, at the baths of Agrippa. Then, after being forced to swim underwater, they were deposited in a fountain

at the end of the *frigidarium* – the large outdoor pool. Three young ladies walking on the grass nearby had nearly fainted at the sight of the youngsters arising from amongst the marble sea nymphs, shaking the water off and strolling towards the exit; but they were revived by one of Nathan's trademark winks.

From the baths, they had made their way watchfully down narrow streets towards the Tiber. They had paused briefly in a quiet cul-de-sac to get their breath back. Here Topaz told them about Jake's note and they had discussed what he might have meant by *I've gone to sort it out*. They had come to the painful conclusion that he had set off to Agata's villa to save Lucius. They had all felt a twinge of apprehension. Topaz, in particular, had felt sick with remorse; she wished she had not scolded him so sternly the night before. After all, it was clear that, while Jake sometimes didn't do the *right* thing, he always did the *brave* thing.

To lighten the mood and keep everyone focused, Charlie had produced his bag of tricks and, after a debate as to who would look better in a black beard (Topaz reluctantly had to concede that it suited her brother better), they prepared to set off again.

'I think Mr Drake may have to stay here . . .' Topaz had pointed out delicately. 'I mean, if we're to keep as low a profile as possible.'

Charlie had not been happy, but of course he saw the logic. He set him carefully on a branch of a nearby pine tree with a handful of peanuts – along with whispered promises to be back soon, which he dearly hoped to keep.

From here they had doubled back along the river, past the temple of Hercules, across the Forum Boarium to the Circus itself.

'Shall we . . .?' said Nathan, cautiously stepping out of the portico and around the perimeter of the square. The others followed, looking around, double checking that no one was following. Once again they joined the stream of people hurrying towards the side entrances.

'The first thing you need to know about the Circus Maximus,' Charlie explained in a low voice, 'is that it is, without question, the prime destination of the Roman world. All roads lead here. From the storm-tossed shores of Hispania in the west to the deserts of Assyria in the east, its fame is un-paralleled. It's epic, heroic, *gargantuan*,' he added, emphasizing each word with a shake of his clenched

fist. 'It is a dream factory. The quintessence of the empire.'

Nathan and Topaz exchanged a knowing glance, enjoying their friend's enthusiasm despite their predicament. Indeed, Charlie was so excited about his visit to the stadium that, for a moment, he forgot about their dire situation: completely in the dark, aware that a catastrophe that could *end dominions* was about to unfold, but knowing nothing of what it might be or when it would take place.

'And the reason it's the prime destination of the Roman world? Well, obviously there's the building itself,' he continued. 'The largest stadium the planet has ever seen, or indeed *will* ever see. Capacity – a hundred and fifty thousand; construction – two hundred thousand tonnes of marble; timber from half a million trees.' The building loomed closer. 'And that's just the current version; in its four-hundred-year history it has already – rather carelessly – been burned down three times. That's why Augustus built this version in marble.' Charlie shook his head. 'So the place itself is a big enough lure, but it's what goes on here that really pulls the crowds.'

'The chariot racing?' Topaz offered.

'That's right. The Romans are fanatically, ridiculously obsessed with it. Obviously loads of other stuff happens here: wild-beast hunts, gladiatorial combat – you know, of course, that the Colosseum won't be built until the end of the century – athletic competitions, even theatrical events and musical recitals. But those are just distractions. The main event, the really big draw, is the chariot racing.'

The hullaballoo coming from the stadium increased, and by the time they had reached the southeastern corner, the roar was deafening – exhilarating and unsettling in equal measure.

They could now see along the side of the building: a vast precipice of arches upon arches upon arches disappearing far into the hazy distance of the city. The people were flocking from all directions, pouring out of every street and passageway; white togas and brown tunics surged into the honeycomb of entrances, chattering excitedly. Some were chanting and singing; others swigging from clay bottles, all cheered on by locals watching from their windows. To add to the cacophony, hundreds of street vendors plied their trade: flower-merchants, incense-sellers, jugglers, fire-eaters, fortune tellers and astrologers.

'It's free, you see, and everyone is invited,' Charlie explained, raising his voice above the clamour. 'And there are games on at least a hundred days of the year. It must be a logistical nightmare!'

Briefly Topaz was separated from the others and had to push her way forward again. Charlie was right: it seemed as if all of Rome was there – men, women, young, old, rich and poor. Throngs of children darted through the crowds, while the old made their way more sedately.

At length the three agents were swept along through an arched entrance and bumped, shoved and elbowed up a winding stone staircase. In the chaos, Topaz couldn't stop thinking about Jake. She was tormented by visions of what Agata, the she-devil, her so-called mother, might do to him.

At the top of the stairs they were jostled forward, and finally squeezed out into the arena. As a wave of cheers echoed around them, Nathan's heart soared and he had to remind himself that the applause wasn't actually for him. He gazed from one end of the Circus to the other, a faint, incredulous smile on his face. Topaz blinked in disbelief, while Charlie stared in awe. In the course of their work for the History Keepers' Secret Service they had seen

countless wonders, but this was perhaps the most astonishing of all.

The arena was almost half a mile long from end to end. A vast man-made basin stretched between the Palatine and the Aventine, whose slopes were also teeming with spectators. There were six levels of seating. The bottom tier, edged by a balustrade and separated from the track by a deep drainage gulley, was the widest and contained the largest quantity of white – the colour worn by the richest citizens. From here the levels rose up, the rake gentle at first, but steepening dramatically towards the top. The higher you went, the noisier and more tightly packed the tiers. Charlie calculated that the top one alone, which looked miles away, must have held more than fifty thousand people. Its colonnade, punctuated by column after column, would have been an incredible structure in its own right, let alone as a crowning afterthought to the rest.

Running down the centre of the arena was the *spina*, the stone island that divided the track in two. 'Grisly fact . . .' Charlie announced. 'According to legend, it was originally made of the crushed bones of Rome's enemies.'

The whole island was teeming with men in

white, purple-edged togas; more were climbing up onto it.

'The senators, I take it?' asked Nathan.

Charlie nodded. 'Whether they like it or not, they're expected to attend. It's considered bad form not to be seen supporting the games.'

'And a no-show would be kind of obvious,' Nathan commented. 'They are rather the centre of attention.' He was right: all eyes were on them, a distinct, bright band of white and purple rising out of the sand. Some of the senators waved at the crowd; others chatted in groups as slaves offered them drinks from silver jugs.

Amongst the throng of senators, the *spina* also sported a number of intriguing monuments: at each end stood clusters of golden spiked cones, three times the size of a human, and, in the centre, a giant Egyptian obelisk. 'Looted from the court of Rameses the Second and now considered one of the wonders of Rome,' Topaz informed the others.

'And the emperor sits there, I take it?' Nathan pointed to the terrace in front of the *pulvinar*, the distinctive temple that jutted out halfway along the track. An empty throne – an enormous seat of white alabaster – was set beneath a bright red

awning. Golden statues of eagles guarded each corner of the terrace, and flames flickered from a host of bronze torches.

'That's right,' Charlie agreed. 'The royal terrace is accessed by its own special passageway, which leads directly from the villas on the Palatine.'

'So they don't have to mix with the riff-raff, I suppose,' Nathan said.

'Let's go then,' suggested Topaz. 'I take it our emperor will be arriving at any minute, so we should approach – with caution of course.' She set off in the direction of the *pulvinar*. Apart from anything else, she needed to get thoughts of Jake out of her head. She kept thinking about Alan and Miriam and how she was going to explain his disappearance. The other two followed, threading their way through the crowd.

Suddenly the three of them were cloaked in shadow; it crept along the tiers of seating, darkening a great swathe of the arena. They looked up to see a roof canopy – a series of long white sails – being drawn across the top of the stadium by a network of ropes. Charlie shook his head and muttered something about the 'stunning technical pizzazz' as the senators in the centre were enveloped in welcome shade.

At the same moment Topaz froze. 'Hydra!' she hissed, and swung the others round just as four soldiers in grey breastplates and bronze masks muscled their way through the crowd, knocking people flying. They marched past and took up positions – a brooding, eagle-eyed group – close to the edge of the emperor's terrace.

'They're everywhere . . .' Nathan nodded towards other soldiers filing towards the *pulvinar*. 'Let's just wait here for the time being,' he murmured, his jaw clenched with frustration.

Lucius's ankle cracked as he landed and he cried out in agony, stumbling down the remainder of the slope. He and Jake had crept across the roofs of Agata's villa, searching for a safe way down. They had chosen a windowless corner next to a cluster of tall pines. Jake had successfully leaped across onto a tree and lowered himself down. Lucius, who could only see out of one eye, and not well from that, had misjudged the jump and tumbled through the branches.

'Yake, I think it is broken,' he said, wincing as he clutched his ankle. They were both in a bad state, scratched and bruised, but Lucius was worse:

not only half blind but cut to ribbons all over.

Jake knelt down and carefully examined Lucius's foot. 'It's badly sprained, but I don't think it's broken,' he said.

'Just leave me – best to leave me, Yake,' Lucius groaned.

'*Ssh.*' Jake put his finger to his lips, aware that they were still in enemy territory. 'You're not getting away from me that easily,' he whispered, smiling. 'I'll help you up. Let's go.' He put his arm round Lucius and slowly hauled him to his feet. 'You see the road there, winding down the hill? We just need to follow it. It'll take us straight there. You don't want to miss the fun, do you?' he joked.

Jake hid his panic well. He knew it was vital to reach the Circus Maximus as soon as possible, but he was simply not prepared to abandon his friend. He had saved Lucius and was determined not to leave him where he might be recaptured. Constantly on the alert for signs of pursuit, Jake helped his companion down the slope towards the Circus.

'There she is,' hissed Nathan, spotting the distinctive figure of Agata Zeldt emerge onto the terrace of the *pulvinar*. Dressed in a plain white

dress, she deliberately hung back in the shadows, watching the crowd through narrowed eyes. Topaz, invisible in the crowd, stared back, and saw a chubby boy with flowers in his fair hair appear behind her.

Nathan did a double-take when he saw him. 'Charlie, am I going insane' – he nudged his friend – 'or does that boy look exactly like that oaf Caspar Isaksen?'

Charlie followed his gaze. 'From Sweden? Don't be ridiculous.' For a moment a group of guards blocked his view. When they moved out of the way, he caught sight of a youth stuffing a cake into his mouth.

'Hell's bells and Bathsheba!' Charlie gasped, barely able to believe his eyes. 'What on earth . . .?' Caspar giggled as Agata whispered something in his ear. 'What *is* he doing here? And with her?'

'It would certainly explain our little mishap in Stockholm,' Nathan commented drily.

'But he's an Isaksen!' Charlie insisted. 'One of the oldest, most revered families of the History Keepers' Secret Service! They go back eight generations.'

'And I'm a Zeldt, theoretically,' Topaz reminded them. 'Loyalty is strange animal.'

On the track, ten men in golden tunics filed out and lined up, their backs to the royal box. As the audience realized that something was about to happen, a great cheer swelled around the stadium. Each man carried a trumpet – a horn curved in the shape of a six. As one, they lifted the mouthpieces to their lips and blew. The blare of sound cut across the clamour.

Nathan and Charlie looked around as the roars of the crowd seemed to suddenly double in volume. A hundred and fifty thousand people had got to their feet and a blizzard of white rained down – pale flowers cast from every corner of the stadium. At first Nathan and Charlie wondered at this, but Topaz nudged them and nodded towards the *pulvinar*. It was no longer empty. The distinctive figure of Tiberius had appeared.

The emperor of Rome – the most powerful man in the world, in his robes of gold and purple. Of course, it was not Tiberius at all, but a second-rate actor from Herculaneum called Austerio. Even from a distance, Topaz, Nathan and Charlie recognized his puffy face. But as he held up his bejewelled hand and gave a regal wave, the crowd let out a tumultuous roar.

Nathan gazed over at the senators' enclosure on the *spina* in front of them. Some of the men waved and bowed towards their leader, but for the most part their smiles were forced.

'Where is that viper Leopardo?' Topaz wondered, her eyes still fixed on the royal box.

But there was no sign of him.

'*Non possum*, Yake.' Lucius sank to the ground, half blocking the busy road and halting the stream of vehicles. Everyone started shouting for them to move out of the way, so Jake quickly scooped him up and dragged him over to the side. It had taken thirty gruelling minutes for them to struggle down the west side of the Palatine, ducking out of the way every time they caught sight of a soldier, but the stadium was now tantalizingly close.

'We're almost there,' Jake said cheerily. 'Can't you hear it?' He put his hand to his ear, listening to the thunderous roar floating across the rooftops.

'Leave me, I beg you,' Lucius insisted. '*Non possum.*'

Jake hesitated. He was beginning to see his friend's logic: they were now a safe distance from the villa and he would be much more effective on his own.

Nearby, a man was roasting meat at a *taberna*. 'Look, I can eat,' Lucius said, his face crinkling into a smile, 'while you save the world.'

Jake bit his lip uncertainly, but time was running out. 'All right, it's a deal,' he said decisively. He pulled Lucius to his feet and helped him over to a bench beside the bar, then scooped up some water from a fountain and offered it to him.

After he had drunk his fill, the soldier looked up at Jake. 'Thank you,' he said quietly.

Impulsively Jake hugged him. 'I'll be back for you, don't worry,' he promised, and tore off down the road, weaving in and out of the carts and litters. He had been so worried about Lucius's injuries that he had forgotten about his own. Now, his bruises throbbed, his cuts stung, he ached all over and felt sick and dizzy.

'I have to find the others,' he muttered to himself. 'They'll be safe, of course they will. I'll find them. We'll defuse the bombs somehow – we'll do it.'

22 SEVEN LAPS TO DOOM

As Austerio seated himself on his alabaster throne, there was another blast of horns. The trumpet players turned and strode around the track towards the grand archway at the southern end. As they did so, a group of figures began to emerge from the opening, as if drawn by the music. The trumpeters turned and marched back along the track, now at the head of a grand procession.

In front were the athletes – young men stripped to the waist, their oiled bodies shining in the sun, each with a crown of laurels in their hair. Next came the cavalry: armoured soldiers on prancing steeds, swords held rigidly in front of their faces. A phalanx of musicians followed: a score each of flute and lyre players. And then the incense carriers bearing fragrant smoking torches. Next a troupe of dancers

appeared: girls and boys in flowing silk, some waving spears, others clattering cymbals. Behind came the *mimi* – performers dressed as Roman gods and heroes: Jupiter, Apollo, Hercules and Odysseus – leading an army of fauns, satyrs and all kinds of mythical creatures.

There was a brief hiatus, and then another surge of applause greeted the entrance of the wild beasts. A dozen plodding elephants preceded a menagerie of lions, tigers, leopards and giant bears. The creatures were tightly leashed and held in check by strapping men in full armour. The sight made Charlie seethe with anger. The beasts and trainers peeled off and headed for the holding pens, through a gate in the centre of the *spina* – except for four brown bears, which were led onto a low plinth in front of the emperor's box and chained up in pairs. An attendant brought a basket of bloody meat, which he prepared to throw to them. One of the huge creatures lifted its head and roared in anticipation – making the crowd cheer again. Austerio looked down and his regal smile tightened a little, as if he was wondering what on earth he had got himself into.

The most deafening hurrah of all was reserved for

the charioteers and their horses. They emerged from the shadow of the grand arch – four stallions pulling each of the eight two-wheeled chariots – and formed a perfect line. The shiny, muscular horses wore extravagant feathered headpieces that matched the clothes of their drivers. These stern-faced men wore coloured tunics and leather gauntlets, and carried a many-tailed whip.

'Each colour represents a different district of the city,' Nathan explained, 'and the competition between the teams is fierce. Disappointed fans have been known to throw themselves onto burning pyres when their teams lose. It's all very Italian.'

Nathan, Charlie and Topaz watched as the eight chariots rolled forward in unison. *Everyone* watched them: the emperor, the senators, and over a hundred thousand others. The charioteers' eyes were hard and determined, their fists clenched tight around their reins. Nathan felt a pang of jealousy. He couldn't imagine anything more exhilarating than a race around the most famous arena in history, cheered on by over a hundred thousand fans.

'Look!' Topaz gasped, nodding down towards the furthest team. Four massive black stallions pulled an ebony chariot, driven by a black-clad charioteer

with a shock of perfectly straight blond hair: Leopardo. Topaz quivered when he postured towards the crowd, chin out, mouth curled in an arrogant snarl. Agata, his proud mother, gave a loud cheer when she saw him.

'What on earth are they up to?' Charlie shook his head in exasperation. 'Don't tell me she's going to have him assassinate the emperor mid race!'

Nathan shrugged. 'I wouldn't put it past them. It's just the sort of stagy melodrama they'd like,' he said – as if *he'd* never been melodramatic in his life.

At this moment Jake staggered, panting with exhaustion, into the half-deserted square behind the arena. Hearing the roars of the crowds, he'd felt a mixture of panic, fear, and strange excitement. He'd attended a handful of football matches in London – one at Wembley – but the sound coming from *this* place was like nothing he'd ever heard before.

Jake peered inside: between the front arches and the twelve that led onto the arena itself, stretching the width of the building, was a wide portico. Here a small army of staff, officials and stable hands were busily preparing for the race. On one side he glimpsed stalls of spare horses and all sorts of

charioteering apparatus. Beyond the pillars of the arches, in the brilliant sunshine, he saw the procession advancing along the track. The bare-chested athletes were coming round the end of the *spina*, starting on their return journey. It was when his eyes followed the dancers, cymbals clashing and ribboned spears held aloft, that Jake suddenly noticed the row of identical objects suspended above the end of the central island.

He stopped breathing.

Eggs. Golden eggs, each the size of a hefty boulder, lined up on a thick bronze rail. *One, two, three . . .* Jake counted them. To be sure, he counted again, his eyes widening in amazement. 'Seven golden eggs,' he murmured in disbelief.

His mind started racing as he began to put the pieces of the puzzle together. He had seen the symbols on Vulcano, then again last night in Agata's war room; the word *Counters* had been written beneath them.

'Lap counters,' Jake said to himself. 'There are seven laps; each one is counted with an egg. They must be shifted along or turned over each time the chariots complete a lap of the circuit.'

He thought back to what Agata had said that

morning: *At the climax of the race, as the seven turns, a fireball, the like of which the world has never seen, will herald the bloodiest revolution of all time.*

Now Jake understood what she meant. 'The seven – the seventh egg . . .' He felt the hairs stand up on the back of his neck. 'It's a detonator! The race ends, and the fireball goes off.' He realized he had only one option. 'I have to stop the race.'

Suddenly, in the area between the arches, there was a commotion. As the chariots peeled away from the end of the procession and entered the arcade, the trainers, assistants and stable hands swept into action: seeing to the horses, adjusting the harnesses, checking the chariot wheels and providing water and refreshments for the drivers.

There was a grinding noise as iron starting gates were secured over each archway. The charioteers began to manoeuvre their vehicles towards their starting positions, one behind every gate, and the trainers gave whispered encouragement or instructions.

As Jake watched, he got another shock. The last in line was Leopardo. He stood in his ebony chariot and flicked his whip, not just at his horses, but at his slaves. Sensing that he was being watched, he

turned, but Jake quickly retreated behind the pillar.

'How do I stop it?' Jake repeated in despair, barely able to think straight.

In the arena, 'Tiberius' stood up and slowly walked to the edge of the terrace. He took out a white handkerchief and held it high in the air, gazing in wonder at the expectant crowd. Austerio had never had such an audience, and he was going to enjoy every minute of it.

Under the portico, the chariots edged forward, the drivers tensely clutching their reins. Leopardo closed his eyes and muttered a prayer.

Finally the emperor lowered the white handkerchief.

The gates sprang open. The chariots took off through the arches in an explosion of dust, and one hundred and twenty-eight hooves thundered down the track. The thousands upon thousands of Romans shouted and waved at them.

Without thinking, Jake dashed through an archway and out onto the track. He felt the ground thumping under his feet. He stopped dead, a solitary figure in the great empty arc of the arena. A huddle of senators standing in front of the

golden eggs squinted down at him in bemusement as he suddenly turned, ran back across the track and in under the portico again.

The trainers and stable hands watched as he marched over to the stall of horses. One was already saddled for a rider, and quietly munching hay when Jake sprang onto its back, grabbed a whip hanging on the wall, dug his heels into its flanks and took off. (Well before Jake had even met the History Keepers, he was a more than competent rider. Old friends of his parents had stables in Kent, and he used to go often with his brother.) There were angry shouts, and men ran forward, trying to block his path, but Jake burst through them, under an archway and out onto the track, following the cloud of dust. He crouched low, and urged his horse into a gallop. It leaped forward, and Jake had to cling on for dear life. In truth, he had no idea what he was doing. He had acted on impulse – some part of his brain telling him that in order to stop the race, he would first need to be *in* the race.

On he flew, his horse relishing the chance to gallop unencumbered by a chariot. The shouting Romans were no more than a roaring sea at the edge of Jake's vision.

Within seconds he was closing on the rear chariot. It was trailing behind, one wheel skewed. Suddenly there was a violent crack, and the wheel took off like a missile. Jake's horse veered aside to avoid it as it spun and bounced up into the screaming crowd.

The vehicle tipped onto its side, sending the charioteer flying into the air and then crashing to the ground. The broken chariot continued without him, the snapped axle gouging a deep trench in the sand. Jake overtook it on the inside, but the four stallions raced on regardless, eyes wild, hooves thumping, feathered headpieces streaming in the wind.

Jake was now approaching the other chariots. In the thick pall of dust, he could barely make out the pounding hooves, flailing limbs and flicking whips. They rounded the sharp bend at the end of the *spina*, bunching perilously close together. The wheel hub of the innermost chariot grated against the marble wall in a shower of sparks. For a moment Jake thought it might tip over, but the driver shifted his weight, and the chariot righted itself and carried on into the far straight.

On the emperor's side of the stadium, frenzied

cheers now went up. The seven remaining chariots sped back towards the twelve arches. As Jake rounded the end of the *spina*, he noticed, above him, another row of large golden counters – these ones shaped like dolphins rather than eggs. Two officials pulled a lever to turn the first on its head; it flashed in the sunlight as it spun round. Jake was aware of their astonished gaze as he passed. It reminded him that what he was doing was madness; he would surely be apprehended at any minute. What was more, the gap between him and the chariots was growing. He carried on regardless: he *had* to find a way to stop them.

Nathan, Charlie and Topaz were tense with anxiety. They had edged closer to the *pulvinar*, each with half an eye trained on its occupants. Caspar had carried on stuffing his face, while Agata Zeldt had sidled forward and positioned herself at the emperor's side – but that was all that had happened.

They had watched the race begin and had noticed a single horseman take off after the chariots. Charlie had been unable to explain who he was. 'Just some lunatic, I guess,' he had murmured. It wasn't until he had rounded the bend and started

galloping in their direction that Topaz began to look more closely. There was something about him that seemed familiar, even from a distance. Slowly, realization dawned on her.

'*Mon dieu!*' she exclaimed. '*C'est lui.* Look' – she grabbed the arms of her companions – 'it's Jake. That's Jake on the horse!' Her initial sense of relief that he was still alive was replaced by utter incomprehension. '*Qu'est-ce qu'il fait ici?*'

'I think the sun must be getting to you,' Nathan drawled as he focused on the rider. All at once he saw that Topaz was right. 'What in God's name . . .?' He trailed off, his jaw hanging open.

'Clever boy,' Charlie stated, the edges of his mouth twitching into a smile. 'I haven't got a clue what he's doing, of course, but he's a clever boy.'

At this moment Jake flew past, far below. Charlie had to stop himself from jumping up and shouting out. Instead he clenched his fists in excitement and murmured to himself, 'He has a plan! Thundering unicorns, he has a plan!'

Nathan shook his head, cautiously peering over at Agata Zeldt and Caspar Isaksen in the *pulvinar*.

Caspar was standing, mouth open, frozen in confusion – he had also seen Jake. Clearly dreading

her reaction, he leaned over and whispered in Agata's ear. As she listened, her sadistic smile turned to an acid scowl and she bared her teeth in fury.

At this moment Charlie and Topaz gasped in unison, their expressions freezing in horror . . .

Jake saw the crash unfold. The seven remaining chariots were bunched together, charging down the home straight, when Leopardo, who was in second place, swerved over and shunted his neighbour into the wall of the *spina*. There was a blaze of sparks as the chariot ricocheted off it. It wobbled, then righted itself. Once again Leopardo sent his chariot slamming into the other. This time his opponent's wheel sheared off and somersaulted into the air over the backs of the horses.

The beasts whinnied in panic as chariot and driver crashed down beside them. The two central ones stumbled, and dragged the others towards the *pulvinar*; then they fell, right in the path of the other teams. The oncoming horses tried to jump over the obstruction, only for their chariots to become entangled and overturn in a screeching chaotic pile, yanking the horses back.

As Jake approached the wreckage, his horse

slowed down and stopped dead, spooked, almost unseating his rider. For a moment Jake took stock, wondering if his mission to stop the race might have already been achieved.

But then he saw that Leopardo had avoided the pile of horses and vehicles and was forging on. A team of greys also managed to free themselves from the ruck and took off after him.

Once again, Jake did not think; he just acted. To his right, a team of bays had also got free, but were now pulling an empty chariot. He twisted round in his saddle and, choosing his moment carefully, threw himself off his horse and onto the chariot. He grabbed the reins and flicked them. The four horses took off, veering round the crash site and accelerating in pursuit of Leopardo and his opponent. The crowd roared in ecstasy, seemingly unaware that a new charioteer had joined the fray, while Agata Zeldt twisted her hands in vexation.

A small army of attendants emerged to remove the jumble of chariots and horses and clear the way for the remaining competitors.

As he urged his horses up the back straight, Jake saw, out of the corner of his eye, the second golden egg being turned on its axis. He held on for dear life:

the chariot was light and springy – made from nothing more than strips of wood and metal braces – and shook with every little bump in the sand. Its two eight-spoked wheels were also wooden, with bronze tyres; a central pole fixed underneath the vehicle connected it to the horses' harnesses.

Suddenly Jake hit a deep furrow and was thrown into the air, losing his footing. He clung onto the reins and managed to land on the very back of the platform, glimpsing the track rush alarmingly beneath his feet. He pulled himself forward, securing the reins around his wrists, and planted his legs firmly. He started to get a feel for it, and accelerated, the wind loud in his ears.

23 FIREBALL ROME

After four nail-biting laps, Jake had not managed to make up any ground at all. He had thought of turning round completely and charging towards the others head on; twice he had attempted this manoeuvre – but the horses had been trained to circle in one direction and did not understand his command. Once they had started galloping, he could barely manage to slow them down. And now the gap between him and the others had widened, and when he passed the end of the *spina* and saw the fifth golden egg being turned, he began to despair. Every part of his body was throbbing with pain; even breathing had become agonizing.

But just when he felt he could go on no longer, something appeared through the dust ahead of him – hazy at first, but gradually coming into focus. It

was the spectre of a man, hovering in the air before him. The uproar around Jake faded away as the figure took shape. His bearing was noble, his smile warm, his eyes bright. It was his brother Philip – not as he was when he disappeared three years ago, but as he would be now: a young man of seventeen. Jake knew that this was simply a mirage, a product of his delirium, but now he felt sure that Philip was alive somewhere, that he was calling him from some dark corner of history. The apparition faded and finally vanished, the eyes lingering a moment longer than the rest.

Once again the thunderous roar of the crowd deafened him – the sound had returned, along with his resolve. If Philip was alive somewhere in this world – somewhere in this multiverse of time – *that* was a reason to go on.

Jake bent his knees and urged his horses on faster. The crowd, sensing his determination, leaped to their feet as he swung round the end of the *spina*, hurtling into the far straight.

Agata Zeldt, no longer keeping a low profile, rushed to the edge of the royal terrace (literally stepping on the toes of the emperor), gaping as Jake advanced. He saw her – a flash of red hair as he flew past.

The ground trembled as he began to catch up with the other two teams. Finally he drew level with the second charioteer, a huge, muscular man with a dark beard and a scarred face, who did not turn to look at Jake, but stared imperiously ahead, using his whip on his straining greys.

Just as Jake overtook on the inside, his opponent suddenly veered over, trying to force Jake against the wall of the *spina*. But he held his ground, and the chariots locked together. Now they went careering off in the other direction, towards the perimeter wall. Jake forced his opponent further and further over, so that his outer wheel dropped into the deep drainage gulley. It screeched along, forcing both chariots almost to a standstill. Suddenly Jake managed to disengage his wheel as his adversary tipped over and fell to the ground.

The roars of the crowd were now at fever pitch. Jake charged on in pursuit of Leopardo's black chariot. As he headed round the *spina* once more, he saw the *sixth* golden egg being turned on its end. One lap to go.

Leopardo finally glanced round and did a double-take when he realized who was behind him. He flicked his whip at Jake, who saw in horror that

each of its tendrils ended in a razor-sharp claw. Jake ducked as it whistled past his head and pierced the flank of one of his stallions. The horse cried out in agony as the razor scoured out a tranche of flesh. Jake seethed with fury, determined to defeat this monster. When Leopardo brought his whip down a second time, Jake seized an end, wrapped it around his hand and yanked, almost dislodging his enemy. But Leopardo pulled back even harder, tightening the leather around Jake's hand.

The Leopard had further tricks up his sleeve: he kicked a lever on the floor of his vehicle, whereupon a series of knives shot out from the hubs of his wheels. He smiled maliciously as he pulled on the whip, dragging Jake's chariot in towards the rotating blades.

Jake was powerless to stop it: the spokes of his wheel splintered, the axle snapped, and the chariot went flying, taking Jake with it. He pressed down and launched himself, somersaulting through the air and landing with a jolt on the shaft of Leopardo's vehicle. He looked down and saw the ground thundering past inches below him.

The crowd was euphoric. Everyone leaped up out of their seats, shrieking with delight – everyone

except Agata, whose nails were digging into her neck. Next to her, Caspar watched in blank confusion.

As Jake picked himself up, balancing precariously on the straining shaft, Leopardo, no longer smiling, drew his sword and slashed out at him. Jake dodged the blade, then lunged forward, taking hold of the boy's wrist and smashing it down on the front of the chariot. As the weapon clattered to the floor, Jake leaped over and head-butted Leopardo; but the savage managed to grab hold of Jake's face. As the black stallions galloped towards the finishing line, Leopardo squeezed tighter and tighter, his fingers digging into Jake's eyes.

Agata felt she could breathe again – but only for a second. Suddenly the horses stumbled over a piece of wreckage. The reins were pulled out of Leopardo's hand. Jake took his chance, and punched him on the chin, then on the cheek – before leaping out and rolling across the sand. For a moment Leopardo teetered drunkenly on. Then the chariot crashed into the wall, and he was hurled out, to land sprawled in the drainage gulley.

The seventh golden egg had still not been turned. Agata's bloodless lips trembled. For a terrible

moment she thought her son was dead, but then he moved his head and tried to lift his arm. She turned, spitting, to two of her guards. 'Help him, you idiots!'

As they made their way down onto the track, Agata noticed three more figures leaping down into the arena: Nathan, Charlie and Topaz. 'Traitors! Witch!' she cried, rounding on the remaining soldiers. 'Kill them!' Her face was purple with fury. 'Kill them all! Hack them to pieces!' So piercing was her cry, Caspar and Austerio put their fingers in their ears and watched as the guards charged down onto the track.

The History Keepers dashed over to Jake. Topaz fell to her knees beside him. 'Jake!' she gasped, cradling his head in her hands. His face was almost unrecognizable, covered as it was with congealed blood, cuts and bruises.

His eyes flickered open, and when he saw the apparition above him, a hazy goddess framed in sunlight, he smiled.

'What were you doing?' she asked in amazement.

'F-fireball,' Jake stammered.

'Fireball?' Nathan asked. 'What fireball?'

Jake gathered his wits. 'Bomb,' he told them.

'Gunpowder. There.' He pointed a bloody finger towards the *spina*. 'The senators . . .' He mimed an explosion with his hands. '*The end of dominions.*'

'There are bombs underneath the *spina*?' Charlie clarified.

Jake nodded, pointing again. 'When the seventh egg is turned.'

A jolt of realization shook them all.

'The plan is to murder the senators,' Charlie exclaimed, 'not the emperor.'

'We have to get them off there . . .' Nathan's brain was already searching for a solution.

Jake reached out for Topaz, clutching her hand. For a second he lost himself in her eyes. They had been cold and hard for so long, but now they seemed to sparkle like they had the day he first met her. 'Lucius is safe,' he said.

Topaz leaned over and kissed him. 'You're astonishing,' she whispered.

'Topaz! Behind you!' Nathan shouted as the guards approached, swords drawn.

Topaz jumped up, drawing her own weapon as she swung round. She fought them off with ruthless precision, Charlie and Nathan quickly coming to her aid. All three were so ablaze with passion, so

sharp with adrenalin, they dispatched the soldiers almost instantly.

Jake felt a warm thrill pulse through him. '*You're astonishing*,' he repeated to himself, and decided that, if he died now, he would die happy.

More soldiers jumped down into the deep gutter to help Leopardo. Though dazed, he had only one thing on his mind: the seventh golden egg. 'On your knees,' he ordered one of the men, who duly bent down. Leopardo used him as a step to clamber back onto the track. But when he emerged into the blazing sun, the whole stadium swam in front of his eyes and he collapsed onto the sand.

Once more the guards pulled him to his feet. He shoved them aside and doggedly limped off towards the golden eggs at the end of the *spina*. 'You will die,' he snarled at the senators. 'All of you will die.'

Agata's eyes widened in alarm as she watched him. 'Darling,' she murmured, 'what are you doing . . .?'

Once again Leopardo's legs gave way; but once again he picked himself up and pressed on.

Nathan realized that he had to act fast. He spun round and tore over to the plinth where the bears were chained up. He picked out a huge joint of meat from the feeding basket and then unshackled

the largest – a great beast covered in scars. Using the meat as bait, he lured the bear along the track towards the steps at the other end of the *spina*. A number of the senators watched in horror as the bear lumbered across the sand towards them, snarling and salivating. Some of them started to edge away and climb down the far side, running for cover.

Agata was not watching them. Her eyes were grimly focused on Leopardo, now climbing up the steps towards the golden eggs. 'Darling' – she shook her head in confusion – 'what are you doing?' She turned on Caspar. 'What is he doing?' He didn't need to answer. Leopardo meant to detonate the bomb himself.

The bear padded along, hypnotized by the smell of the bloody meat. Suddenly it lunged towards it – but, like a bullfighter, Nathan twisted it out of reach. The great beast reared up on its hind legs, growling in fury.

The watching crowd were once again on their feet, thrilled by this unexpected twist to the games.

Now Leopardo had reached the top of the steps and was staggering towards the row of eggs. His expression was so murderous that the counting officials fled into the throng. He stepped onto the

plinth and reached up for the last egg. The metal, scorching hot from the sun, burned his hand as he touched it.

Realizing that there was no time left, Nathan swung round and hurled the joint of meat. It spiralled through the air, flicking a helix of blood in all directions, towards the heart of the *spina*. A group of senators watched in astonishment as it spun down towards them. They parted, and it landed with a crunch on the stone. The bear took off after it, bounding up the steps. In unison, six hundred senators sent up a howl of terror, and started throwing themselves over the parapet, a great sea of white and purple pouring down onto the track; it spread across the stadium like a giant flower suddenly opening its petals. The bear was big and clumsy, and struggled to climb the narrow stairs towards its prey.

Ignoring the intense heat, Leopardo reached again for the egg, but was now jostled backwards by the surge of senators. He hissed with rage as he pushed his way through them. He gritted his teeth and stretched out his hand. 'I do this for history!' he cried, and this time he swung the egg decisively on its axis.

'No!' Agata gasped, her eyes wide.

But there was no explosion. Leopardo had not turned the egg fully round. For a moment he stared at it in bafflement. All around him men were fleeing in panic as the bear went to collect its prize. Leopardo was oblivious, his mind fixed on one thing only. Once again he thrust up his hand and turned the egg.

This time the mechanism clicked into place.

Agata stopped breathing, her gaping mouth frozen.

Jake noticed a strange silence, as if everything was suddenly muffled. Then his ears popped, he heard the boom and felt the wave of intense heat. There was a flash, and Jake saw Leopardo take off into the air. He looked graceful, almost balletic, even as his head came away from his body.

'Noooooooo!' his mother wailed, her face lit up by the explosion.

There was a great *crack!* Then the end of the *spina* collapsed in on itself, the three black marble cones falling like skittles. Animals began to pour out of the wreckage: tigers, lions and leopards. The bear that had charged onto the platform had stopped in its tracks, the meat hanging from his mouth. It too

leaped off the *spina*, crashing down into a cloud of dust. The whole auditorium stood frozen in bewilderment.

More explosions followed, one by one, across the central island, hurling volleys of rock into the air. The giant obelisk teetered back and forth, there was a grinding sound, and it too tumbled onto its side. The inferno was extraordinary, spectacular, the flames even brighter than the sun overhead. Wave after wave of heat rolled over Jake and his companions.

Screams rang out around the stadium as people rushed for the exits, the weak and old pushed aside and trampled in the frenzy. Thick smoke covered the track. The animals, some injured and howling with pain, emerged from it, along with choking, shell-shocked senators. One had lost his arm and was searching around for it, and several lay on the sand, lifeless. But most of them had survived the explosion and were climbing up into the auditorium.

'They're going,' Caspar mumbled to Agata, a piece of cake hanging out of his mouth. 'Should they be going?'

Agata wrung her hands, snarling like a wildcat as she glared down at the History Keepers.

Coughing in the smoke, Topaz was collecting the swords of the vanquished soldiers as Nathan and Charlie helped Jake to his feet.

'How many times do I have to ask?' Agata screeched at the last of her retinue. 'Kill them! Kill them all. Kill my daughter!'

The soldiers edged away from her: they were reluctant to go down onto the track and face the wild beasts. A lion was eating a severed hand, while a tiger was standing, roaring, over a still white bundle, the body of a senator.

Then Agata noticed Austerio, his face flushed with panic, mumbling to himself as he made to escape. She intercepted him and slapped his face.

'You belong to me, you toad,' she hissed, dragging him back to the throne by his ear. 'You do what I tell you!'

The poor actor cowered away from her, tears streaming down his cheeks. 'I can't work like this,' he blubbed. 'I have a very low tolerance to danger. I switch off at the merest hint of it.'

Agata set about him, venting the full force of her rage. He covered his head with his hands, begging for mercy, as she pummelled and punched him.

Seeing what was happening, Charlie immediately

spotted an opportunity. He jumped up onto the balustrade and, motioning towards the stricken Austerio, shouted at the top of his voice that the emperor was in danger: '*Imperator in periculo est! Imperator in periculo est.*'

The noise in the auditorium was such that only a handful of people heard him to begin with. But when they grasped what was taking place on the imperial terrace, they turned to their neighbours, pointing. First astonishment, then anger swept through the crowd. Already convinced that some deadly uprising was afoot, the mob surged towards their emperor.

Caspar gulped when he saw them, and tugged at Agata's gown. She stopped hitting Austerio, and turned to see a mass of people approaching, shaking their fists. She held up her hand and, in a thunderous voice, commanded them to stop, but they ignored her.

Agata realized that she had run out of time. She let go of Austerio, dropping him like a sack of rubbish; then turned and threw open the double doors of the *pulvinar*. For a second she looked back at the seething ocean of people; at the smoking ruin of the *spina*; at the broken, bloody pieces on the far

side of the arena that had once been her son. Three tigers were circling them, licking their lips.

Agata snarled defiantly. 'Let ignorance kill you,' she shouted at the people, and disappeared into the building. Caspar and the remainder of the guards followed, slamming the doors behind them.

Nathan was the first to jump up onto the terrace. Charlie and Topaz helped Jake up after him.

Still trembling, Austerio peeked through his fingers. On recognizing the agents, he sat up, shaking his head in wonder. 'My fans,' he sobbed. 'Come to save Austerio!'

'That's right,' Nathan deadpanned, heading straight past him and throwing his weight against the doors. 'Just in time for the finale.'

Charlie went to help him, and eventually they broke through.

'Shall we?' Nathan asked, turning to the others.

Topaz looked at Jake. 'You stay here – it's safer.'

'You think I'm going to leave you now?' he cried.

The four young agents stepped through the doorway.

'Wait for me!' Austerio called, rushing after them. 'Don't leave me with this rabble.'

Inside was a square white chamber lined with

statues and lit by smoky braziers attached to the wall. At the back stood five soldiers, guarding the entrance to the long tunnel into the Palatine. As they spotted the intruders, they raised their weapons – but there was uncertainty in their eyes.

'Really, boys' – Nathan smirked – 'you have to know that the game's up now!'

One of the guards reached for his silver bracelet, but Nathan was ahead of him. He sent his dagger flying through the air towards a brazier. It sliced through the tether attaching it to the ceiling, and burning embers tipped out onto the man's head. The remaining soldiers rushed forward to help him, but tripped on the hot coals. In a breathtaking series of moves, Nathan disarmed the first man with a clean cut, paralysed the second with a crack of his elbow and flattened the third by toppling a marble bust of Augustus onto his head.

'Are *we* allowed to play?' Charlie asked wryly as all four agents closed in on the remaining soldier, who pointed his sword at each of them in turn, and cursed.

'Hot potato.' Charlie winked, scooping a coal up with the point of his sword and flicking it neatly into the folds of the guard's tunic.

As the man hopped around in panic, Austerio

stepped forward. 'What a drama,' he commented drily, shooting out his belly and sending the soldier crashing into the wall. 'You see?' he said, pouting. 'Not just a pretty face.'

'Let's go!' Nathan ordered, and the five of them rushed along the passage in pursuit of Agata, their footsteps echoing loudly. At the end, far in the distance, they saw a rectangle of light that blinked as two figures cut across it. The four agents quickened their pace, Austerio wheezing as he tried to keep up.

It seemed an age before they reached the light, but suddenly they saw a staircase lit by brilliant sunshine. Nathan peered up and signalled for the others to follow quietly. Weapons held at the ready, they cautiously ascended.

They emerged into a tropical garden filled with brightly coloured flowers. Jake recognized it from early that morning – he had seen it from the room where he had learned of Agata's diabolical plans. It was deserted, and Nathan led the way through the trees towards an archway.

They headed through into the arena where the party had taken place. It looked different in the daylight, empty and quiet but for the trickling of the fountains. Suddenly, from above, they heard a

curious *whoomph*, and a huge shape rose high over the garden. Jake stared up in puzzlement, but Charlie recognized it immediately.

'The balloon!' he exclaimed. 'Agata must be escaping in it.'

He was right – it was swaying to and fro, nearly inflated.

They tore over to the door next to the statue of Saturn. Nathan still had the key, and he hurriedly unlocked it. They all dived through and charged up the spiralling steps – one flight, two, three . . . At the top, Nathan headed through another door.

At that very moment the balloon took off, Agata and Caspar ensconced in the basket, the former clutching a veneered wooden box, her pet falcon clinging to her shoulder. As the canopy filled to capacity, lifting them into the sky, all four History Keepers launched themselves towards it, each grabbing one of the ropes that hung down.

Under their weight, the balloon dropped back to earth. Agata reacted instantly: with a flick of her sword, she sliced through Charlie's rope, then Nathan's. The balloon took off again, Jake still hanging from one side, Topaz from the other.

Agata looked down at her daughter and their eyes

locked. There was so much history between them. Agata's sword hovered, its point an inch from Topaz's eye: she could run her through and never hear from her again. But she stopped herself. Just one word came from her lips: 'Ungrateful . . .' Then she hacked the rope in two. Topaz plunged down, her dress billowing in the wind. Nathan and Charlie rushed forward and managed to catch her.

'Jake!' Topaz called as the balloon suddenly surged up again.

Jake's stomach lurched as he saw the whole of Rome spread out at his feet. With grim determination, while Agata was distracted watching Topaz, he pulled himself up to the edge of the basket and grabbed hold of Caspar's toga. Jake felt his sweaty belly wobbling as he gave a high-pitched giggle.

'I've said it once, I'll say it again,' Caspar jeered. 'You and your family are the stupidest people in history.'

Jake clung on, his eyes fixed on the wooden box in Agata's hands.

'I'm going to enjoy your death . . .' Caspar produced a dagger with one hand and grabbed Jake by the neck with the other. Agata's falcon fluttered agitatedly about the basket.

Jake looked down again. He was so high above the terrace that Topaz and the others were now nothing more than moving dots.

'Goodbye, Jake,' said Caspar and brought the weapon down.

The blade flashed, but it never reached its target.

Everything seemed to happen in slow motion. The malicious glint in Caspar's eye froze, replaced by a look of confusion. He cried out as Agata leaned forward and, with one hand, tipped him over the edge of the basket, intending to rid herself of both boys at once. Caspar's dagger dropped from his grasp; but for a second he clung on, staring up at her in amazed horror.

'You're weighing me down,' she said, peeling his fat fingers off, one by one.

Suddenly there came a piercing squawk as the falcon accidentally singed its wing on the burner. It flapped crazily in Agata's face. As she swiped it away, she dropped the box onto the floor. Jake saw his chance, lunged over the edge and snatched it. At the same moment Caspar lost his grip on the basket. He fell, but grabbed onto Jake's clothes first, his weight pulling them both down. They plummeted, clothes flapping, locked in a tangle of limbs. The ground

shot up to meet them. Caspar hit the terrace first, cracking the marble. Jake landed on top of him, his fall cushioned by the other boy's big belly.

For a moment Caspar stared up stupidly, watching the balloon soar away across the city, realizing that he had been abandoned.

Jake rolled off onto his knees and held out the box. Nathan grabbed it, opened it and smiled. Inside were two full vials of atomium – the same bottles that had been stolen in Stockholm.

They turned to look at Caspar. 'I can't feel anything,' he murmured, suddenly frightened. He tried to lift his hand. 'Why can't I feel anything?' A pool of blood was spreading out from beneath him across the white marble. He looked at them all in turn. Even in this state, his crafty mind was still working. 'Maybe I went a little too far . . .' He tried to smile. 'Agata Zeldt brainwashes you, you must realize . . .' He stopped. 'Why's it going dark?' he panted.

'Caspar,' said Jake, 'you have to tell me – have you seen my brother?'

'I don't have to do anything for you . . . It's as black as pitch!' he cried, his body shaking, his face pale.

'Answer me!' Jake persisted. 'Philip – did you see him? Tell me!'

'Yes, I've seen him,' Caspar sneered. 'I even tortured him. But I expect he's dead by now.' He tried to laugh. 'He thought you'd forgotten all about him . . . *The History Keepers*.' He spat out the words. 'You're all amateurs.'

Jake shook him. 'Where have you seen him?' he demanded desperately.

'Such terrible darkness,' Caspar sighed. Then his eyes froze and he was still.

'Where have you seen him?' Jake wailed again. But Caspar was gone – along with everything he knew. 'Where? Where?' Jake sobbed. Topaz threw her arms around him and held him tight. Nathan and Charlie looked at each other sombrely.

Agata's balloon floated off into the distance, climbing higher into the hot afternoon sky. In every street, the traffic stopped and the people looked up, struck dumb by the apparition floating noiselessly overhead. It drifted northwestwards over the Circus Maximus; over the Field of Mars, the Tiber Island and the watermills of Trastevere. It crested the great Gianicolo hill and vanished from sight.

24 A PLACE IN HISTORY

Nathan and Charlie solemnly covered up Caspar's body. He may have been a traitor but everyone was filled with remorse. He had, after all, once been one of them, a History Keeper, and from one of the noblest families of all.

Removing his corpse was not practical; but after they had crept down the stairs and evaded the remaining guards, they went straight to an undertaker's – a *libitinarius* – that Charlie had noticed in a row of shops at the foot of the Palatine. Here they spoke to a cheerless, gaunt man (Jake wondered why funeral directors invariably looked half-dead themselves), and left money and instructions for a full ceremony. They knew that at some stage they would have to meet Caspar's family; they wanted to reassure them that he had been buried with dignity.

The next stop was the *taberna* where Jake had left Lucius. As they made their way through the traffic, Topaz nervously quickened her pace. When she saw him sitting by the bar, she rushed forward, took his bloody face in her hands and kissed him. Jake stopped and looked at them both. He found that he was no longer jealous but proud, for in his own way he had brought them back together again.

Nathan and Charlie went off to collect Mr Drake from his hiding place (the parrot was so delighted that he hadn't been left behind after all, he completely forgot to be angry with his master), and then on to the Forum Boarium, hoping to find someone to take them back to Ostia, where the *Conqueror* was docked.

Their timing couldn't have been better: Gaius, the blind perfumier, had sold all his stock, and was inundated with orders from affluent housewives. In short, he needed to return to his home town urgently to make more. Charlie and Nathan were only too happy to help him out. They boarded the cart with the old man (it was much more spacious without the jars), went to pick up the others at the *taberna*, and the whole troupe, Austerio included, set off on the journey back to Ostia.

As they trundled up the Caelian, Jake looked back at the metropolis below, at the sun setting over the Circus Maximus. The stadium was empty of spectators, but an army of workmen was already clearing away the rubble of the *spina*, ready to reassemble it. 'It's not the first time it has been rebuilt,' Charlie said, 'nor will it be the last. They'll make it better, stronger, even more majestic than before.'

As they rounded the summit, Gaius started singing. Austerio joined in, and Lucius too. Although they didn't know the words, the others also started humming the tune; even Nathan – who usually hated sing-alongs – was unable to resist. Jake took one last look at Rome, now a mass of twinkling lights in the dusk below, before it vanished from sight.

He lay back, looked up at the ultramarine sky and thought back to the events of the day: the escape from Agata's aviary, the chariot race around the Circus Maximus, the bombs, the wild beasts, the hot-air balloon (he shuddered at the thought that he might have died five times over) and, finally, the sensational news that Philip had been seen alive.

Alive.

Yes, I've seen him, Caspar had sneered. Wonderful news – even though his later sentence seemed to banish that hope again: *But I expect he's dead by now* – and, worst of all: *He thought you'd forgotten all about him*. Never. Philip would *never* be forgotten.

Jake looked up as the first stars blinked in the heavens and decided that, for tonight at any rate, Philip *was* alive – that the apparition he had seen in the arena was somehow a guarantee that he existed somewhere in the world, at some time in history. With that, a strange peace came over Jake and he fell into a deep sleep.

He was awoken in the middle of the night by Topaz and Lucius talking in hushed whispers.

'I don't understand,' Lucius was saying. 'Why do you have to leave?'

Topaz searched for the right words. 'Lucius, I . . . I come from a different part of the world, far, far away from here. And I have to go back . . . It is my duty,' she added solemnly.

'Duty?' Jake could hear Lucius's voice crack with emotion. 'Is there someone else you love?'

'I suppose . . . there are many things. It is almost impossible to explain – it's a question of honour.'

There was a long silence before Lucius said, 'I wanted to build a house by the sea for you.'

Jake opened his eyes slightly and saw that Topaz was stroking his face, a tear rolling down her cheek.

'We'll make sure you're safe,' she said. 'That you have somewhere to go.'

They said no more. She held onto Lucius's arm tightly as the cart trundled along through the night.

It was when they were arriving in Ostia the following morning that Jake suddenly had a brainwave about Lucius. (The idea that the Roman had lost everything – not only his job, but Topaz too – was dreadful. In fact, the subject had been on everyone's minds.) Jake remembered the story that Nathan had told him on their way to Rome – about Gaius's unfortunate history.

He turned to his friend. 'You said that before Gaius lost his sight, he used to be a carpenter, didn't you?'

'What of it?' the American replied.

'Well, maybe the old man knows someone who can help Lucius find a job. He also comes from a family of carpenters. His father used to repair boats.'

Nathan pondered for a moment, then smiled

broadly. 'Jake Djones, you really are a genius. I'll broach the subject.'

When Nathan really wanted to be civil, there was no one more charming or helpful. He took Gaius and Lucius to one side and the plan was embraced with enthusiasm. Soon the pair were shaking hands while Gaius's dog barked and jumped around for joy. It turned out that Gaius knew lots of people who could employ Lucius; moreover, he still had his old workshop and would be delighted if his new friend could make use of it. He added with a twinkle that his town was full of beautiful young ladies.

On hearing this Topaz grimaced a little and looked down at her feet. And Lucius, always the gentleman, came and put his arm round her.

It was not easy to say goodbye. While Charlie went to buy some provisions for the journey and Nathan and Jake returned to ready the *Conqueror* for the voyage to Messina (via Herculaneum, to drop off Austerio), Topaz and Lucius wandered along the quay. They bought some fruit and sat on a low wall, watching the ships come and go. Lucius got down on one knee in a last vain attempt to persuade Topaz to stay with him. In the end,

however, they both returned to the ship looking miserable.

Lucius gave everyone a hug – holding onto Jake for a full minute before whispering in his ear, 'I hope you find your brother, Yake.'

'I hope you find yours,' Jake replied earnestly.

'Look after yourself. I will never forget you. Not as long as I live.'

Lucius and Topaz shared a final sad embrace, then the four History Keepers – and Austerio – boarded the ship and cast off.

Jake and Topaz stood side by side at the stern, staring back at the dwindling figures of Lucius and Gaius. Jake remembered the story Rose had told him on their way there – how she had fallen in love with a farmer in Peru. *Of course, it's hopeless falling for a civilian*, she had sighed, *because they can't go back with you. It's hard enough explaining you live on the other side of the world, let alone the other end of history.* Jake said nothing to Topaz, but reached out and took her hand. It was warm, soft, trembling. She squeezed Jake's fingers and a lump went down her throat.

Austerio was tremendously excited by the speed at which the ship tore across the sea, and kept

offering up theatrical blessings to Neptune. At Herculaneum, they accompanied him to the theatre and he bade them a dramatic farewell – before being reunited with his long-lost 'enemy', Fico the Fantastic. On seeing the two actors together for the first time, it was quite clear to everyone that in fact they were utterly devoted to one another.

When the youngsters reached the open sea again, Nathan appeared at Jake's side with the sword that he had confiscated. 'I believe this belongs to you,' he said. It was the weapon with the dragon hilt that Nathan had presented to him at Point Zero. Luckily Jake had left it in the Roman bureau, accidentally taking Nathan's, when he had rushed off on his crazy mission.

'Thank you,' he said, taking it gratefully. Then he added with a timid smile, 'I've learned a lesson or two.'

'The truth is, we all get carried away from time to time,' Nathan said. 'At a ball once in Habsburg, Vienna, I thought I could carry off skin-tight leopard print. I was the laughing stock of the city.' His tone became more serious. 'Every one of us is hot-headed from time to time – even Charlie has his moments.'

They headed south for Messina, and before long

sighted the hills of the large island. Just before they had set off, Nathan had sent a Meslith to Point Zero, informing the commander of their progress. They, in turn, had contacted Rose and Jupitus, who were standing very close together on the quay when the *Conqueror* arrived.

Jake jumped ashore before they had even docked, and gave his aunt a great hug. She pretended to be horrified by all his cuts and bruises but really felt quite proud. Jupitus waved at another ship along the quay, announcing that the *Hippocampus* was fully operational again and that they should all set sail immediately. Then he gathered up his crutches, limped over and struggled aboard alone.

'You two getting on all right?' Jake asked tentatively.

Rose grinned. 'Surprisingly well. Why don't you come with us and tell me all about your adventures?'

When Jake had first seen the *Hippocampus* at Point Zero, he'd felt sure that he'd seen it before. As he climbed aboard now, he had the same sensation: its sun-bleached timbers, its sails of cream and blue stripes were still familiar.

Both ships set off across the bay side by side. Within minutes they had rounded the lighthouse

and were heading for the open sea.

Rose appeared from below with a tray of tea and biscuits. 'Refreshments . . .' She handed a cup to Jupitus. He took it, barely raising a smile; then Rose and Jake sat down cross-legged and started dunking their biscuits.

'Why do I recognize this ship?' Jake asked.

'What's that, darling?'

'I feel like I know it somehow – even the name . . .'

Rose was one of those people who could neither lie nor keep a secret without blushing or becoming twitchy. She was now doing both: fiddling with her teacup as her cheeks went red. Jake examined her suspiciously, making her even more self-conscious.

'You know something, don't you? There *is* a reason the ship's familiar . . . When I asked Mum and Dad about it before, they started behaving oddly too.'

'I'm not behaving oddly,' she insisted.

'Rose, you've gone pink.'

'Drat! I'll get into such trouble if I say anything. Your parents have sworn me to secrecy.'

'So there *is* a secret!'

Rose took a slurp of tea and munched a biscuit, wondering what to do. Finally she sighed. 'Well, I suppose you were going to find out soon enough.'

Jake felt a thrill of excitement, as if he were about to hear something momentous. He was not disappointed. Rose looked round and checked that Jupitus wasn't listening, then leaned in close. 'You *have* sailed on this ship before, a number of times . . . when you were a baby.'

'A baby?' gasped Jake. 'I don't understand.'

'When you were very young,' she whispered, 'your parents and I took some trips on it together, as a family. Alan, Miriam, me, you . . . Philip.' And now the bombshell: 'The last time was Persia, 1327—'

'Persia? 1327?' Jake stammered.

'I remember because your mother had terrible toothache,' Rose reflected.

Jake had to get up and go to the rail to take some calming breaths. 'So I've been to history before?'

'Just a couple of times – before we all gave it up. It seemed wrong to leave you at home. And you were no trouble at all. Spent most of the time sleeping.'

Jake laughed.

'I suppose you'll have to tell your mum and dad I let the secret slip. No doubt I'll be in the dog house.'

At length the passengers on both ships took their doses of atomium in preparation for the horizon point. After the appalling outward journey, Jake braced himself for more of the same. But, although it was as dramatic, with the same amazing out-of-body experience, he didn't suffer any horrific hallucinations. They vaulted all the way to the Atlantic, to an entry point in the Bay of Biscay, just west of La Rochelle. It was getting dark by the time that Jake spied the conical shape of the Mont St Michel in the distance.

Ever since Rose's confession, Jake's mind had been working overtime, mulling over the information that he had already travelled into deep history as a young child. He had asked her a number of other questions but, making sure that Jupitus wasn't within earshot, she insisted that his parents should fill him in on the rest. Now he clung to the rail at the prow of the *Hippocampus*, willing her on. He had so much to say to his parents – not just about Rose's revelation, but about Philip.

So when the ship docked just behind the

Conqueror, to an enthusiastic welcome, Jake was the first to disembark, running down the gangplank towards his parents.

'Heaven's above! What have they done to you?' asked Miriam. Like Rose, she was taken aback by the damage to his face.

'Miriam, that's no way to greet him.' Alan pinched Jake's cheek. 'This is what an adventurer looks like.'

Jake was about to blurt out his news, when Jupitus suddenly gave an urgent cry. 'Foreign craft approaching!' Everyone turned at once.

Another ship, its slanting sails silhouetted in the twilight, was cutting across the sea towards them. Instinctively the whole group huddled together as Galliana quickly produced a telescope from her belt and examined the vessel.

'It's Chinese,' she said, sounding equally alarmed.

'Should we arm ourselves?' asked Jupitus.

It was enough for Oceane to clutch at her pearls and retreat into the safety of the castle, pulling Josephine along behind her.

Galliana continued to stare through her telescope, examining the occupants of the craft. She could make out six silhouettes, standing at the prow. 'I've

seen this ship before. It belongs to the Chinese bureau.' Then, as she identified one of the passengers, she relaxed. 'That is Madame Tieng, no question.'

There was a communal sigh of relief.

'Are you sure?' asked Jupitus.

Galliana nodded. 'She is smiling at me.'

'Who is Madame Tieng?' Jake asked.

'She's the commander's counterpart in Peking,' whispered Miriam. 'A formidable lady. But what on earth is she doing here?'

Eventually the ship docked, a gangplank was lowered and the travellers nervously filed down onto the pier; distinguished-looking men and women, all dressed in exquisite Chinese clothes. Jake noticed there were no youngsters amongst them – they were mostly Galliana's age. They shivered in the brisk Atlantic wind. The ladies looked like rare flowers imported from some exotic clime.

Madame Tieng, a striking white-haired woman with black eyes and rosebud lips, stepped forward and bowed to Galliana.

'We escaped in the dead of night,' she informed her. 'The Chinese bureau has been ransacked.'

'Ransacked?' Galliana asked, trying hard to hold onto her emotions. 'By whom?'

Madame Tieng looked up at her. She shook her head and closed her eyes. 'By Xi Xiang's men,' she said. 'I sent a young team in search of him, but I believe we are all now in danger.'

There was a horrified gasp. Jake had no idea who Xi Xiang was, but it was clear from the hurried, nervous conversations that another mission would soon be sanctioned, perhaps to the east – maybe to China itself. He already longed to be part of it. His father was right: he was an adventurer, it was in his blood. He was a History Keeper – surely he had proved that now. And, after all, he had travelled to history as a baby.

He turned round and locked eyes with Topaz; then both of them looked out to sea. Jake thought again of his brother Philip. The Atlantic breeze seemed to stir his heart.

'You're alive,' he murmured as it ruffled his hair. 'I know you are out there . . .'

ACKNOWLEDGEMENTS

Once again I would like to thank the five wise goddesses: Jo Unwin, Becky Stradwick, Sue Cook, Sophie Nelson and Lauren Bennett for all their incredible work and never-ending support. And, of course, Ali Lowry for being his fantastic self.

Finally I would like to dedicate this book to my brother Justin, and to Berne, Lukas and Zak – in memory of Justine, a wonderful and inspiring lady, who will never be forgotten.